Alicia Keys, Ashanti, Beyoncé, Destiny's Child, Jennifer Lopez & Mya

Divas of the New Millennium

By Stacy-Deanne, Kelly Kenyatta, Natasha Lowery
with Contributing Writer Kwynn Sanders

Compiled and Edited by Kwynn Sanders

COLOSSUS BOOKS

Phoenix

New York   Los Angeles

Alicia Keys, Ashanti, Beyoncé, Destiny's Child, Jennifer Lopez & Mya

Divas of the New Millennium

By Stacy-Deanne, Kelly Kenyatta, Natasha Lowery
with Contributing Writer Kwynn Sanders

Compiled and Edited by Kwynn Sanders

COLOSSUS BOOKS

Phoenix
New York   Los Angeles

Alicia Keys, Ashanti, Beyoncé, Destiny's Child, Jennifer Lopez & Mya
Divas Of The New Millennium

By Stacey-Deanne, Kelly Kenyatta, Natasha Lowery with Contributing Writer
Kwynn Sanders
Published by:
Colossus Books
A Division of Amber Communications Group, Inc.
1334 East Chandler Boulevard, Suite 5-D67
Phoenix, Z 85048
amberbk@aol.com
WWW.AMBERBOOKS.COM

Tony Rose, Publisher/Editorial Director   Samuel P. Peabody, Associate Publisher
Yvonne Rose, Senior Editor   The Printed Page, Interior & Cover Design
Compiled and Edited by Kwynn Sanders

© Copyright 2005 by Stacy-Deanne Reed, Joyce Kelly,
Natasha Lowery and Amber Communications Group, Inc.

ISBN13: 978-0-9749779-6-6 / ISBN 10: 0-9749779-6-9

Library of Congress
Catalog-in-Publication Information Pending
2005

About the Authors

Stacy-Deanne

Born in 1978 in Houston, Texas, Stacy-Deanne (Dee-Anne) is a writer of fiction and celebrity biographies. The author of *Ashanti, Jennifer Lopez* and *Mya*, Stacy-Deanne's hobbies include part-time modeling and landscape photography. She's also certified in Editing. She resides in Houston, Texas. You can learn more about Stacy and upcoming releases by visiting her official website – www.stacy-deanne.net

Kelly Kenyatta

Kelly Kenyatta is a Chicago-based writer and freelance journalist and holds a bachelor's and a master's degree in journalism. The author of *Destiny's Child*, Ms. Kenyatta has written for numerous publications including: Black Enterprise magazine, People magazine, the *Chicago Tribune, The Los Angeles Times* and the *Indianapolis Star News*. She is also the author of *Destiny's Child Complete Story; The Collector's Edition: Yes, Yes, Yes: The Unauthorized Biography of Destiny's Child (The Story of the Original 4 Members); You Forgot About Dre—The Unauthorized Biography of Dr. Dre and Eminem and Aaliyah: An R & B Princess—in Words and Pictures*.

Natasha Lowery

Natasha Lowery is the author of *Alicia Keys*. Ms. Lowery has an MFA in creative writing from the City College of New York. She has a BA in English from Fordham University. She is a native New Yorker who lived in Harlem for over 17 years. The *Alicia Keys Unauthorized Biography* is her first non-fiction work. Natasha is single and resides in Teaneck, New Jersey. She is now working on her first fiction novel.

Kwynn Sanders

Kwynn Sanders, contributing writer and editor, and author of *Beyoncé's, Kelly's*, and *Michelle's stories*. Ms. Sanders is a freelance journalist and editor residing in Pittsburg, California. She has a Bachelor's degree in English from Vanderbilt University. *Divas of The New Millennium* is Ms. Sanders first published work.

Contents

Introduction

As a genre, Hip-Hop music took off in the early 80's and has never set foot back on ground. A type of music that no one thought had any staying power has been extremely popular for over 20 years, and continues to rule the airwaves today. Despite the negative publicity that often surrounds Hip-Hop, the music is more present than ever; it has been transformed from an inner-city music form into a sound that the general public encounters every day. The music is constantly evolving, keeping the sound fresh, and lengthening the categories that are listed under the title.

One of Hip-Hop's greatest successes has been fusing two different forms of music, thereby creating a new sound and widening its audience. Over the years, we have heard Hip-Hop and disco, Hip-Hop and rock, and Hip-Hop and reggae all combined to create a unique and distinct sound. However, one of the longest-running and most embraced infusions is the combination of Hip-Hop and R&B music. In fact, this duo has become so popular that it has created its own sub-category that is now recognized at all music awards shows.

Although represented by all, R&B/Hip-Hop singers and audiences are dominated mostly by young African-American women. One would think that women of color, having the opportunity to be such a dominant force in society would be a completely positive step in the direction of equality; however, as the years have passed, this domination has been replaced with degradation.

Today, many talented women are being turned away from record companies because a beautiful voice is simply not enough. Women today must also have an image, and in today's world, that image must be sexy. The problem is that many acts embrace an exaggerated sexuality and not only lose the public's respect by doing so, but more importantly, lose themselves in the process. What these women do not realize is that having class and dignity is what truly makes a person sexy, not the clothes that they wear or how well they wear them. Thus, we, the audience, are bombarded with oversexed acts that have no staying power due to a lack in talent. The most unfortunate issue is that besides setting women back decades, this action harms the self-esteem of the women of the future, because they feel that they have to be nearly naked to be desired or have worth.

Luckily, there are women in the R&B/Hip-Hop community that realize this issue, and therefore attempt to change these images by showing audiences that although a woman should cherish her sexuality, it is a quality that is inherent in *all* women. These women have more pride in the thing that sets them apart from every other woman in the world: their talent…their ability to make people dance to their music and sing along to their songs. These divas of the new millennium realize that their music will have a longer lasting effect on people than their physical characteristics, and adversely, the artists themselves have a longer lasting effect on the public, because audiences recognize and appreciate their talent.

Mya, Alicia Keys, Jennifer Lopez, the women of Destiny's Child, and Ashanti are some of today's musical pioneers who are striving to regain respect, dignity and self-esteem for all women. These talented women of color have achieved record-breaking and groundbreaking successes all while remaining true to their community, their fans, and most importantly, themselves.

Kwynn Sanders
May, 2005

Alicia Keys

Alicia Keys

Thousands of people gathered in Times Square on September 5, 2002 to celebrate the start of the NFL season as well as the strength and determination of New Yorkers nearly one year after the horrific events of September 11, 2001. The first game of the NFL season was to be amplified by the music of superstars, Jon Bon Jovi, Enrique Iglesias, Eve, and Alicia Keys.

Although all of the performers and Americans held a special adoration for New York in light of the recent events, the evening was especially meaningful for Alicia. This performance was much more than a season opener, it was her homecoming.

Today, anyone walking through New York's "Hell's Kitchen" area would wonder how it earned such an unworthy name. It is enviably comprised of small eclectic boutiques, varieties of cultural cafes, and high-rise apartments that can compete with any upper eastside address. However, this diverse area, only walking distance from Times Square, has been beautifully refaced since Alicia Keys grew as a child there.

Alicia recalls the streets of Hell's Kitchen to be dripping with scantily clad working ladies, quarter private peep shows, drug dealers, and number runners. However, she attributes her humility to growing up in these "real" surroundings, and is grateful that she had the positive influence of her mother to guide her away from those irreverent activities.

𝒯rack 1: "𝒴ou 𝒟on't 𝒦now 𝒮y 𝒮ame"

On January 25, 1980, Terri Augello, an Italian-American struggling actress and paralegal gave birth to Alicia Augello Cook. Although Alicia was not raised by her African-American father, Craig Cook, Terri encouraged her to embrace both sides of her ethnicity. Terri also convinced Alicia to take an interest in having an assorted taste in people and creative arts. With this direction, it was only a matter of time before Alicia began her innovative journey.

Alicia first awed audiences at age four when she exhibited her mature vocal ability during an audition for her kindergarten's play, *The Wizard of Oz*. It was at this moment that Alicia's mother realized how talented her daughter was, and how serious Alicia was about performing.

Alicia began taking piano lessons at age seven from teacher, Margaret Pine, who marveled over Alicia's talent in *Vibe Magazine* when she said, "Even from a young age, Alicia had stage

presence... At one of her early recitals she played Chopin's 'Raindrop Prelude', and the audience went crazy...You felt like she threw her whole heart into playing it." It was not long before this activity outweighed all other extra-curricular activities.

She did find time however, to join an all girls group called "EmBishion". The group's vocal coach knew that he had discovered something special in Alicia and introduced her to his brother Jeff, an R&B manager. He immediately agreed to manage the young talent. By the time Alicia was of high school age, she had mastered the difficult Suzuki piano playing method and was ready to enter the prestigious Professional Performing Arts School.

Alicia Cook felt that her name was rather plain and would not stand out against others as she prepared to pursue her musical career on a professional level. She knew that her talent was in a class of its own, but she wanted her name to stand out and be as memorable as her musical skills. She needed a name that was not only catchy, but also that was descriptive of her as an individual. After tossing out several horrible names such as "Alicia Wild", she finally settled on "Alicia Keys".

Alicia's mother continued to support her child's budding talent, but was also smart enough to forewarn her of the difficulties she would encounter in the entertainment business. As a struggling actress, she had faced many of her own disappointments and wanted to make sure that Alicia was prepared for the hardships she was destined to encounter. Alicia heeded her mother's warnings with a receptive ear and patiently continued to perfect her craft.

♈rack 2: "ℭaged ♉ird"

Since Alicia's childhood, her mother had always encouraged her to believe in herself as an individual and also as an artist. For this, Alicia was confident with her talent and knew that her dedicated practicing would eventually yield professional success. At age fifteen, she was not completely shocked when she landed a record deal with Columbia Records.

She did not go to Columbia Records empty handed, however, as many new artists do, bringing only a shoddy demo tape; Alicia brought along a demo filled with original pieces that she had written and composed, including *Butterflyz* and *The Life,* which would eventually be used on her debut album. She found it very important to demonstrate to the label how involved she was in every aspect of her music.

However, Columbia thought differently. The executives at the label, according to Alicia "didn't like what [she] did" and thought that her music "sounded like one long demo". The

label further attempted to constrict Alicia's artistic freedom by suggesting that she change her look in order to broaden her appeal.

Alicia's mother had taught her to respect her individuality and never compromise herself. She knew that losing herself for the gain of a record deal would mean losing her own self-respect. She found this to be a harder fate to deal with than the possibility of missing out on stardom.

Luckily, Alicia realized early on that her career would move slowly if she stayed at Columbia. She felt that her artistic freedom was being intruded upon, and found that she and Columbia Records were not the best fit. Unfortunately, she was bound to a contract.

Alicia focused on high school, and at age sixteen she had graduated as a valedictorian and received a scholarship from Columbia University. Her college career only lasted one month as she abandoned Columbia to pursue her life's calling,

making it the second "Columbia" that did not fit in her life's plan.

She saw that her good decision-making and dedication to her craft had paid off when she met the music industry's most respected and sought after talent scout and hit maker, Clive Davis. He had discovered some of the most talented musicians in their genre, including Janis Joplin, Bruce Springsteen, Carlos Santana, and Whitney Houston.

At age nineteen, Clive added Alicia to his list of hit makers when he bought out her contract from Columbia Records. As his tenured musical career with Arista Records came to and end, he started his own label, J records; he felt that with his new protégé, the company was guaranteed to succeed. Likewise, Alicia knew that with Clive's direction she was destined for a fantastic career.

Track 3: "Piano And I"

Alicia's first album, *Songs in A Minor,* was released on January 26th, 2000, only one day after her twentieth birthday. The single "Fallin" received fair radio play, but Clive wanted to really launch her sales. Clive put her in an arena that any struggling artist can ensure an overnight boost in appeal and sales: *The Oprah Winfrey Show.*

In front of 40 million people, Alicia belted out her hit single "Fallin". Although she was in the presence in such a remarkable and impressionable woman, Alicia kept her urban image the same. She wore her signature braids, sat at the piano, and shared her beautiful fusion of classical music and soul with an audience who normally would not have experienced it. Alicia's appearance on the show, as expected, set her career into motion, and her album shipment doubled over the next week.

Alicia admired Clive as a businessman and producer, but she truly respected him for a different reason. Clive allowed her to truly showcase her musical talent and gave her artistic license to do so. She verbalized her appreciation when she said, "[Clive] didn't try to divert me into something else. I wanted to be who I am. I didn't want to be made into what somebody else thinks I should be."

Alicia only hoped that he could allow her to maintain her individuality while he molded her into a woman that would change the face of music—just as he had done with veterans Janis Joplin and Whitney Houston.

Track 4: "Feeling You, Feeling Me"

Alicia's musical style was just as eclectic as her Hell's Kitchen neighborhood had become. Her classical training served as her disciplined side of the music, while the soulful aspect allowed her to experiment with her artistic freedom. Alicia's unique sound was created as she united her various loves: she bound the structure of Mozart with the natural freedom of Aretha Franklin, social consciousness of Marvin Gaye, and the innovativeness of Prince. She completed her sound by evoking the emotion of Mary J. Blige into each one of her songs. By emulating the best artists in each genre, she perfected her own sound.

From this well-measured combination, Alicia truly touched her audience. Her music stirred sentiments in her fans that they had been unable to put into words. Audience responses to her music ranged from giving a simple head nod in agreement to fully throwing their hands in the air admitting that they whole-heartedly related to what she was talking about.

Alicia further showed appreciation for her one of her mentors when she remade Prince's "How Come You Don't Call Me Anymore" on *Songs in A Minor*. As we all know, imitation is the best form of flattery, and Alicia's interpretation of the song caused audiences to gain a new respect for the original, which had not gained much recognition when initially released.

Her appreciation for Prince was deeper-rooted than respecting his music; she valued him as an artist and as an individual. He was a composer, producer, dancer, singer, actor, as well as sex symbol. In her eyes, Prince was the true definition of an artist. He loved his art and did not concern himself with the opinions of critics. This was the quality that Alicia truly wished to evoke in her career.

As Alicia grew as an artist, she realized what an integral part Hip-Hop played in her music. Hip-Hop thrived on originality and heart, and Alicia's music strongly emanated each of these attributes. Unlike many other artists, Alicia did not have a separate public and personal persona; she was always herself. She—like true Hip-Hop—was always real.

Track 5: "So Simple"

It was this sense of "realness" that made many believe that Alicia was wise beyond her years. It was hard for the public to believe that a person who was a mere twenty-one-years-old could know and understand so much about life's trials and hardships. Although still the age of a young adult, Alicia was presented to the world as a mature woman.

Alicia always took life seriously. She truly listened to the astute advice her mother had given her throughout her life. She used her surroundings in "Hell's Kitchen" as a barometer to gauge the things that she treasured against the activities in which she did not want to become involved. She remained consistent with honing her musical skills, while maintaining an A average in school.

She did not expect for her career in music to be any different. Although past record executives had tried to market Alicia's beauty, she felt that it had nothing to do with her talent as a musician. She saw that the industry had begun to produce a barrage of musical clones whose talent came second to their aesthetic appeal.

Alicia was careful not to fall into this category, and found it essential to present herself in a different manner. She understood her responsibility to today's youth, and was very conscious

of how impressionable and susceptible to self-esteem issues this group was.

The infiltration of videos in the music industry had only heightened the amount of sexual titillation that many artists were exhibiting. Unfortunately, "good video" had far too commonly become synonymous with "sexy video". Alicia realized that whether she wanted the responsibility or not, she was a role model to younger audiences.

Despite her sudden rise to stardom, Alicia did not suddenly decided to "sex up" her image as most starts did; instead, she

15

continued to focus on her art, and stayed true to herself and her growing fan base.

Track 6: "A Woman's Worth"

As Alicia's acclaim continued to grow, the United States was hit with an unforgivable blow. The first attack ever on American soil occurred as New York's World Trade Center towers crumbled to the ground. Although the country was devastated and at a standstill, Alicia was expected to continue promoting her album.

Songs in A Minor had sold more than three million copies in nine months and she signed on to tour as an opening act with Maxwell as well as posing for several photo shoots. However, she found it difficult to enjoy her success due to the drastic events that had just occurred. She found it particularly hard to continue with her everyday life when her photo shoot for *Rolling Stone Magazine* was located only a block away from the rubble.

Alicia took the attacks personally; she *was* New York. She had grown up only a few miles from the World Trade Center and the area was a part of her everyday life. Somehow, she was able to evoke the strength of her city and herself on the *Rolling Stone* cover; she posed in a New York City midriff shirt with her arm raised in a position ensuring that she, and the city, would remain strong regardless of any hardships thrown their way.

Alicia continued to exemplify her knowledge of hardships in real life situations with the release of her second song "A Woman's Worth". Again, she managed to amaze audiences with her maturity by capturing the challenges and victories of relationships in her music.

She preached to men about valuing their women, and assured women that it was sometimes acceptable to be vulnerable to their emotions. She praised some men for seeing the true worth in their women while scolding others for being neglectful and selfish. For many fans, she had become a musical relationship therapist.

It was at this time that the public began to question Alicia's own intimate relationships. She did not discuss her personal life in detail, and due to the fact that she was not seen exhibiting her femininity in a stereotypical way—such as wearing gowns and heavy make-up—ignorant audiences labeled her as a lesbian.

Alicia, cool as always, responded to the speculation in *Vibe Magazine* by saying, "Why? 'Cause I'm assertive? 'Cause I don't wear dresses? Give me a break; it's silly." And to this day, Alicia still refuses to discuss her relationships—even though she has reportedly been with the same man for five years. She had learned to value privacy long before Jennifer Lopez set an example of what *not* to do as a celebrity in a relationship.

Furthermore, Alicia showed that femininity could not be merely defined as what clothes and accessories a woman wears. True femininity was strength, and demanding respect for yourself as a woman. Femininity was understanding and supporting your fellow sisters. Femininity was being proud of your sexuality, but being in control of it. Femininity was feminism.

Alicia was truly a modern day feminist. She remained strong and knew that her diligence would dispel any ill-crafted rumors. Music lovers dismissed the claims and continued embracing her music as record sales reached ten million. Critics catapulted the album's success by nominating it for several Grammy Awards.

Track 7: "Karma"

Alicia was awarded a recognition she never expected as she received six nods at the 2001 Grammy Awards. Her stiffest competition would be fellow newcomer India Arie, who like Alicia, shot to success after a performance on *The Oprah Winfrey Show,* and had received seven Grammy nominations. Also like Alicia, she was a singer/song-writer who reveled in her natural beauty and played an instrument.

Despite the escalated anxiety that the media had created, Alicia was remarkably cool that evening. Perhaps she simply knew that she had nothing to worry about. Alicia's name was called five times out of six throughout that evening as she won awards for "Best New Artist", "Best R&B Album", "Best Female R&B Vocal Performance", "Best R&B Song", and "Song of the Year" for 'Fallin'.

Although she did not appear nervous during the show, she was stunned by the show of support and love from fans and other artists. Even India Arie, who did not win a single Grammy despite her seven nominations, showed respect and love for her rival by congratulating Alicia on her impressive feat. She tied Lauryn

Hill's 1999 Grammy winning record and realized that this was the moment she had always anticipated: she had come full-circle as an artist.

After experiencing such dramatic success with *Songs in A Minor*, Alicia decided that she needed time to relax before starting a new musical effort. As a songwriter, she also needed time to compile more material. However, this did not stop other artists from seeking out Alicia's talent.

Eve approached Alicia about embarking on a collaborative effort with her, and what was born was the hit "Gangsta Lovin". The song was a widespread success and the sexy but genuine duo pushed the track to the top of all charts. The song had such mass appeal that the two were asked to perform it at the NFL's season kickoff in Time's Square. Alicia officially had her city, and the nation for that matter, under her control.

Alicia's knack for writing and producing music attracted other A-list artists, such as Christina Aguilera. Alicia had recently started her production company, Krucial Keys Enterprises, with Kerry "Krucial" Brothers, and Christina asked Alicia to help her write and produce a single on her upcoming album. Although Keys was just winding down from her year in the spotlight, she liked the idea of working with the little lady with a powerful voice. Without further contemplation she produced the single "Impossible". Christina experienced first hand what a perfectionist Alicia was as the recording of the song was taped on an episode of MTV's *Diary*.

She then decided that she would find true peace in fulfilling her philanthropic responsibilities, and began to use her celebrity to speak out on important issues. Her concern with the increasing number of youth diagnosed with AIDS led her all the way to the Africa. On December 1, 2002, Alicia, along with fellow musicians, such as rap mogul and entrepreneur P. Diddy, participated in World AIDS Day in Capetown, South Africa. Alicia performed and promoted the importance of safe sex.

Yet, it was more than just an opportunity for Alicia to perform; it was an opportunity for Alicia to educate the young population about AIDS as well as be educated herself by people dealing with the disease on a daily basis.

This journey changed her views about life and the disease forever. Alicia was so emotionally touched by the people, especially the small smiling children infected with HIV, that she promised to do more. She had already witnessed many friends dying from AIDS; therefore, she knew that merely loaning her face to a promotional ad would not be enough.

Alicia's close friend and pioneer of AIDS awareness, Leigh Blake, knew Alicia was one artist who would actually get even more involved. Alicia didn't need a lot of coaxing. She spoke along with Stephen Lewis, one of the world's greatest speakers on AIDS, and blew the audience away with sentiments that came straight from

her heart. In an interview with *Vogue Magazine,* Blake compared Alicia to one of the world's most loved philanthropists when she said, "Lewis and all of us were blown away by the words that were coming from this young girl's mouth. You can put her with absolutely anybody and she's like Princess Di—she finds a way to connect."

It instantly became apparent to Leigh that since Alicia shared the same intense passion for putting a stop to AIDS as she did for her music, she should be the new spokesperson for her charity, "Keep a Child Alive." Alicia proved that anyone could make the time to give back.

ϙrack 8: "Ᏽeartburn"

After 22 months away from her own music, Alicia decided that she had rested enough and had gained enough material to begin producing her second album.

It was not long before Alicia released her sophomore album, *The Diary of Alicia Keys;* with its release, she invited her fans to experience her views on relationships in a more personal manner than ever before. *The Diary of Alicia Keys* was the highest debuting album of any female artist in 2003.

Similarly, the debut single "You Don't Know My Name" was an instant success and it quickly rose to top spots on both contemporary and R&B charts. She again used her successful fusion process to meld old school R&B with the sounds of today's Hip-Hop/ R&B. The song gained its authenticity from the help of legendary R&B group, "The Moments", who ensured that the song emitted a smooth and nostalgic feeling. Alicia knew how important it was to pay homage to artists that had paved the way for such young talents as herself.

She further showed appreciation to an old school artist that had particularly affected her love for music and the piano when she performed alongside Stevie Wonder at the 2004 MTV Music Awards. Besides respecting Stevie as a musical genius, she directly related to the former child prodigy who had a talent for song writing and playing the piano. The surprise performance, also featuring Lenny Kravitz, was the highlight of the entire awards ceremony.

Fans were very pleased with Alicia's sophomore effort, and were excited that she had proven her longevity as an artist. She proved to the world that a second album can be just as good as a five-time-Grammy-award-winning first, if not better. The album rose to a triple-platinum status and sold an outstanding

168,000 copies within its first week. She had done what many artists were incapable of: she sounded like a veteran at the young age of twenty-two.

Alicia continued to differentiate herself from other R&B song-stresses when she maintained the persona she had established on her first album. Unlike other artists who strive to make a statement with their sophomore projects by revamping their images, Alicia's image remained the same, but had simply matured.

She experienced continued chart-topping success with her releases of "Diary" and "Karma", and showed her eternal love for New York, as well as her step up in celebrity status, as she fea-tured rappers Mos Def and Method Man as her love interests in the "You Don't Know My Name" and "If I Ain't Got You" videos, respectively. Both of these men are well known among true Hip-Hop fans and emanate the feeling of New York and all that the culture encompasses.

The album continued to gain momentum, and she was congratulated with multiple award nominations, including six Grammy Awards, eleven Billboard Awards, and 4 Vibe Awards in 2005. She won the AMA for "Favorite Female Artist" in the Soul/R&B category.

In addition to the hits that she released from her own album, she achieved a long-running success when she combined her talents with 2004's top hit-maker Usher Raymond. Usher released several versions of "My Boo", but it was the version with Alicia Keys that was the most popular. The steamy video and their friendly relationship aside from the song sparked rumors that the two, who have known each other since they were teenagers, were an item. Both sides assured the interested public that they were only friends.

Track 9: "The Life"

Alicia's gain in celebrity status was not only apparent by who she shared her videos with, but also by who she shared the stage

with. She enlisted in being one of three female acts at the Verizon's Ladies First Tour in the spring of 2004, when she shared top-billing with superstar headliners Missy Elliot and Beyoncé Knowles. The three proved to be the perfect mixture of talent, confidence, and sex appeal as the concert sold its capacity in each city's venue.

Alicia herself was impressed with her fans at the concerts as fans sang along with her hits from *Songs in A Minor*, and listened intently to the songs from the newly released *Diary of Alicia Keys*. In return, Alicia impressed the audience with her piano playing stunts and impressive vocals. What was the most impressive to the audience was Alicia's willingness to let her three background singers shine.

During a brief portion of the show Alicia left the stage, leaving her background singers to entertain the audience. They were incredible, and each singer had the ability to carry the show him/herself. Though the performances were abbreviated, the audience became aware of what an unselfish artist Alicia was. While most artists would be afraid of being upstaged at their own show, Alicia proved her respect and appreciation for good music while sharing her spotlight with other possible up-and-coming artists.

It is this humility that greatly contributes to Alicia's untouchable success. She still lives in the same house in Queens, NY where she spends a great majority of time writing her hits. She maintains a close relationship with her mother, and has ensured the time they spend together by employing Terry as her personal assistant. She still eats at her favorite vegetarian restaurant and continues to enjoy New York without a huge entourage of friends and bodyguards. From Alicia's down-to-earth actions, one would not know what an important icon she is.

On the other hand, producers and publishers are fully aware of Alicia's celebrity, and they intend to market off of the fact that the public cannot get enough of Alicia Keys. She has been approached with several movie scripts, and while she has not agreed to any to date, she expressed an interest in appearing in a small production, and working her way up to bigger roles.

She also showed her interest in the literary world, as she signed a deal to write two books available in fall 2005: *Songbook,* a collection of poetry and lyrics, and *The Diary of Alicia Keys,* a biography. As the public is infinitely interested in Alicia's life, the two are destined to be best sellers.

Besides her personal marketing endeavors, Alicia continues to pay respect and stay involved in bettering life's plights. She is scheduled to perform "America the Beautiful" at the 39th Super

Bowl, accompanied by 150 students from the Florida School for the Deaf and Blind. The patriotic song, which has only been performed three times at the NFL ending game, was chosen to pay respect to Ray Charles, the man who made it his own while performing it the first time at the Super Bowl. Alicia is flattered that she is able to again pay homage to another musical genius.

She continues her philanthropic efforts as she promotes AIDS awareness and raises funds with charity UNAIDS.

She sees the bigger picture behind the camera flashes, smiles, and platinum records. Instead of using her celebrity to gain access to the hippest nightclubs, she is more interested in exploiting it for the welfare of humankind. Respectably, Alicia truly desires and aspires to make the world a better place.

And even today, despite her enormous record sales and infinite music nominations, she is still in awe when people know all the words to her songs.

Some critics have even labeled her with the self-important title of "mogul", and to that statement, Alicia responded, "That's something that's going to happen over a long period of time and continue happening through my 50's and 60's. From the beginning, I've realized how important it is to be a part of as many things as you can. Not just out front, but behind the scenes. Be the creator, the producer, and the writer. It gives you freedom, more of a say, and a greater voice. And, I want to have the biggest voice I can possibly have."

Alicia has not yet realized that her voice has been loud and has been heard clearly since the debut of her first album; and, her voice continues to boom with each project she embarks on. Whether it be a hit single or AIDS advocacy, Alicia's voice is big; but she never imagined that millions of fans would be singing right along with her.

Ashanti

Ashanti

One of the most difficult dilemmas in the lives of young people today is that our role models mainly consist of entertainers. While many entertainers are fully capable of being positive role models, a problem exists in the fact that the public is only introduced to these performers once they have made it. We are disillusioned about the let downs, the set backs, and the rigorous processes that entertainers endure to gain fame and success. Most notably, most of today's youth fails to recognize the sheer determination needed to reach their role model's level of success.

Ashanti Douglas' story is an insight on how one truly achieves fame and success. Ashanti's accomplishments did not occur overnight; she struggled for over ten years to make her mark in the entertainment field. However, Ashanti will be the first to tell you that all of the struggles and stress that she suffered were well worth it.

Track 1: "Dreams"

Kincaid Douglas and his wife Tina worked hard for years trying to balance their dreams against the struggles of making ends meet. Both worked long hours in a hospital in order to survive, but Kincaid felt he belonged on stage. In his free time, Kincaid sang with a band while Tina taught dance at a local

dance school. Tina's true talent lay within her ability to spot a gift in the people she taught.

At one point, it seemed they had no room for much else; yet, they were aware of the sacrifices they would have to make when Tina became pregnant with her first child. Ashanti Shequoiya Douglas was born on October 13, 1980, in Glen Cove, New York. The Douglas' welcomed their second daughter, Shia, ten years later.

Tina's father, James, had a deep connection with Ashanti from the moment he laid eyes on her. As she grew to a toddler, Ashanti followed James everywhere he went; the two became inseparable. James took on the role of the "third parent", and Ashanti considered her grandfather to be her best friend. Like his daughter Tina, James possessed the gift of seeing hidden talent in people, and he spotted Ashanti's gift instantly. He knew that she would become something that no one ever imagined.

Track 2: "Black Child"

Ashanti was not an easy child to keep up with; in fact, she was a handful. She couldn't sit still and she always wanted to be center of attention. She was not shy; she loved to sing, dance, and perform gymnastics for anyone willing to watch.

After four years of dealing with Ashanti's tiresome hyperactive personality, Tina decided that she needed to channel her child's energy. She enrolled Ashanti in dance classes at the dance school in which she taught. Tina wasn't sure if structure would hold Ashanti's interest or enthusiasm, but thankfully, it did.

Ashanti learned discipline. She built stamina and learned how to behave through dance. On Saturdays, she was at the dance school for at least eight hours at a time, taking her own jazz and modern dance classes, and then waiting for her mother to finish her classes. Spending so much time together at the dance school only strengthened the bond between the mother and daughter. However, it did not leave much time for Ashanti to have a social life with her own peers; thus, Ashanti decided to balance dancing with running track.

Her neighborhood had created a platform for the children to run amateur track. The runners were mostly boys and were very fast. This did not discourage Ashanti from competing in the races, and it did not take long before she had beaten many of these speedy males.

Of course, in the beginning, many of the young boys' egos were bruised, and they resorted to calling Ashanti names in order to deal with their emotions. Nonetheless, Ashanti did not allow this to affect her, and she continued to race against and beat these boys. As time passed, they had no choice but to respect her.

Once she had beaten the competition and gained their respect, she was ready to learn from them. She found that she enjoyed the company of boys better than girls. She loved competition—a contest in which boys were always involved. Before long, she became "one of the boys", and it would not be much longer until she realized what an important attribute this would be in her life.

Dancing and running track didn't diminish Ashanti's interest in singing. By age six Ashanti got a chance to sing in front of an audience that wasn't made up of only family members and friends when she started singing at church. Her voice wasn't fully developed at the time, but her enthusiasm helped make up for what she lacked in development.

Ashanti got bored with activities quickly, so Tina decided to further stimulate her by introducing her to modeling. She felt Ashanti was too striking to hide from the world, and she also believed that it would be great exposure for her daughter. When Tina could not attend auditions with Ashanti, grandfather Jimmy was more than happy to fill in. If her audition did not go smoothly, he would not leave her side (sometimes staying for hours) until she assured him that she was okay. As a result, their

relationship deepened, and Ashanti began to confide in and rely on her grandfather as her support system.

The support provided by her family and her own perseverance paid off as she was awarded a role in 1989's *Polly*. The movie was a remake of the 1960 all-white production, *Pollyanna*. *Polly* was an upbeat, urban version of the film directed by famed dancer Debbie Allen. The film which also starred "The Cosby Show's Keisha Knight Pulliam and Phylicia Rashad became one of the year's most entertaining television events.

This led her to work under the Black Spectrum Theater, a theater company dedicated to helping the performing arts careers of African-American children. She also began training at the Bernice Johnson Cultural Arts Center in order to take her dancing skills to a more noticeable level, and went on to showcase her talents with the Brooklyn Academy of Music. Ashanti then experienced the opportunity of a lifetime as she accepted a part with the Alvin Ailey Dance Company.

𝔗rack 3: "𝔥appy"

Ashanti fell more in love with entertaining each time she had the chance to perform. For quite some time, she enjoyed dancing more than singing. However, when she uncovered the writing aspect of singing, the balance shifted.

Ashanti had no trouble conquering her English classes and became an honor student. As her need for writing grew, she became more determined in pursuing a singing career.

Ashanti's interests changed. The stage, in the context that she knew it, grew less intriguing. She appreciated and valued her training, yet she couldn't contain her intense fascination with the sounds of the latest-recording artists. Ashanti wanted to sing professionally.

Luckily, Ashanti had never been a person who was afraid to take chances. Tina learned of Ashanti's improved vocal talents and sudden ambition when she was twelve. The rule in the Douglas household was no music while doing household chores. Tina told Ashanti to turn the radio off and was stunned to discover that the beautiful voice she heard was not the radio, but Ashanti herself.

Tina's mind churned. She felt that Ashanti's talent outweighed everything else about her, including her beauty. She knew that Ashanti could go far with hard work. Tina and Ashanti immediately began making demo tapes for record companies and choreographing the best dance steps to showcase Ashanti's style. Through all of this, Tina stressed the importance of Ashanti's individuality. Tina taught Ashanti to focus on her own creativity in order to show future record executives that she was unique, and had something different from present singers.

Ashanti studied vocal combinations and performed singing sessions in front of the video camera. The process was very strenuous and time consuming, yet Ashanti didn't mind spending her spare time to make tapes.

During this procedure, Ashanti experienced a small sample of how hard working in the music industry would be. Yet, she was still naïve about one of the most strenuous difficulties she would soon encounter—landing a record deal.

Track 4: "Feel So Good"

Around the time R&B hottie Aaliyah ditched her deal with Jive Records, Jive searched for a fresh face. Ashanti had found her opening. After reviewing Ashanti in 1994, Jive decided that she was exactly what they were looking for. Ashanti had so much excited anticipation that she did not even share her accomplishment with her friends for fear of jinxing her luck.

Her schedule suddenly became even more hectic as she spent long evenings in the studio after her school days at Glen Cove High School. She had given up the chance to lead the normal teenage life, and had transformed into an adult with responsibilities over night.

She had to work extremely hard to maintain her grades. She had to do her homework anywhere she could fit the time, including in the car or at school before she headed off. Ashanti's long days turned into longer nights. She worked at the studio until the wee hours of the morning and somehow managed to squeeze in a few hours of sleep before heading to school.

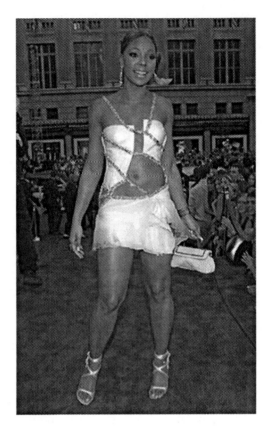

Ashanti eventually became frustrated with Jive when she felt that her input was not being taken into consideration. She found that the company had their own ideas about the direction of her album and what her image should be. Jive was trying to fashion her after the mold of a pop-singer; this idea went against everything her mother had ever taught her about valuing her individuality.

It didn't take long for Ashanti and Tina to realize that the music business was not compassionate when it came to new artists. Ashanti and Jive split after two years of trying to develop a solid relationship. Ashanti's disappointment was heightened by the fact that she was a teenager. She was ultimately devastated that all of her time and hard work had not come to fruition.

Ashanti relied on her family to help her through the sad time. She reclaimed her closeness with Jimmy who did all he could to comfort her. Ashanti became educated with the way of the world while spending time with Jimmy. Her grandfather helped her see that she wasn't only special, but that she also had something many kids did not. She learned that just because an opportunity passed didn't mean she had to give up on her dream.

Ashanti decided to take what life gave her. She put performing on hold to become a schoolgirl again. She concentrated on school in order to take her mind off of the disappointment and participated in several after-school assemblies and programs, including track and cheerleading. She also continued to maintain her impressive grade point average. As always, Ashanti continued to stand out in groups; she was always the participant that had the spark, or player that left the audience breathless.

She became a local celebrity in Glen Cove due to her winning record on the track team. Though a decade had passed since she first took an interest in running, she was still one of the fastest women on the Glen Cove Varsity track team. She is still known in Glen Cove for her triple jump record. Ashanti found it fulfilling to delve into other activities, and the pain of disappointment disappeared one day at a time.

She began receiving attention from Princeton and Hampton University, and decided that she wanted to pursue a law degree while in college. However, although Ashanti had regained her self-esteem and rerouted her aspirations by the time she graduated from high school in 1998, the urge to pursue music was stronger than ever.

Track 5: "Leaving (Always On Time Part 2)"

The strange intricacies of life are forever present. Just as soon as Ashanti had decided to move away from music, a record company approached to reel her back in. Epic's Noontime Records had heard Ashanti's demo tapes, and offered her a contract as she was contemplating a career in law. Ashanti was shocked and unsure of how she should feel. It wasn't easy to revisit that chapter of her life.

She talked at length with her parents about her next step, and everyone decided that it would be best for Ashanti to take advantage of this opportunity that had presented itself again.

The enjoyment that singing gave her was nonequivalent to any other activity she had ever engaged in.

Ashanti and her parents even felt that they were at an advantage this time around, because they now had first-hand knowledge of the music industry. In spite of this, they were all shocked when Noontime told Ashanti that she had to move to Atlanta to record her album. Begrudgingly, she left her family in New York to pursue her career in Georgia.

Ashanti felt terribly alone and frightened. She was only eighteen, and didn't know if she could succeed on her own. Her fears drastically decreased when she received a warm welcome at Noontime.

The company treated her as though she were a rare jewel that they were lucky enough to stumble upon, and wanted to make sure that they kept her happy. She stressed her concerns about creative control the first day she arrived in the studio. Noontime was happy to oblige.

She again began recording her debut album, and found that she preferred recording in a dimly lit booth. Sometimes she sang in near darkness, with a mere candle or lamp as her light source. The production of the album was progressing at an impressive pace, and it only awaited a few finishing touches when everything fell to pieces.

A mysterious, undercover deal took place, and a new manager emerged from Epic. The new manager's ideas about the company did not coincide with the ideas of previous manager. The new manager not only had his own creative outlook and expectations, but he also brought his own acts to the company. Of course this meant that there was not much room for previous artists, and many of these acts did not fit his expectation anyway.

Ashanti was unaware of what was happening, but she knew that something was wrong when her album's release date continued to be postponed. She would go to the studio to record only to be told that she was not recording that day. Her work was suddenly put on hold without warning, and eventually, Noontime told Ashanti that she no longer needed to come to the studio.

Track 6: "Foolish"

Ashanti hit rock bottom. She felt she didn't have the talent to become a star; all of the esteem her family had instilled in her vanished. She had no expectations, but worse, she had no hope. Ashanti became dangerously depressed and despondent. She didn't know many people in Atlanta, but those that tried to see her were turned away.

Ashanti stayed locked in her home and didn't leave for weeks at a time. She found comfort in eating, watching television and solitude. She shut down from the world and everyone around her. It was the first time in her life that Ashanti had been *this* miserable. Her negative experience with Jive had been hard to bear, but her family's support had quickly nursed her through her disdain; this time around, she had no one.

When Ashanti did leave her home, she relied on the Atlanta nightlife to console her. She partied hard and went to numerous nightclubs to ease the pain. This only served as a temporary bandage, because she would again become upset the minute she returned home. She deeply regretted many of the choices she had made in her life.

Ashanti fought depression in Atlanta while her family worried about her back in Glen Cove. She desperately wanted to go back to her family, but it was not until she was involved in a near fatal car accident that she actually took action on her desires, and moved back to New York.

Ashanti returned to a life in which she had grown unaccustomed. Everyone her age was enjoying their start in the "real" world. Some of her peers were married or had children while others were packing to go to college.

As people began to probe about her singing career, Ashanti found herself too embarrassed to explain that her record deal had fallen through again. She opted to avoid the questioning by hiding in her house.

As Ashanti continued to question her talent and reexamine her dreams, she was unaware that the very thing that had torn down her self-esteem twice would be the same thing that helped her regain her sanity.

Track 7: "Carry On"

Singing soothed Ashanti when private talks with friends and family failed. Ashanti began to write songs to quiet her soul,

and soon saw that it became her outlet when no one else really understood her.

She was careful not to lose any idea, jotting down everything that came to her mind—even if it was only one lyric. Unlike other songwriters, she never allowed songs to "breathe"; instead she had set a strict writing schedule for herself. Yet, as structured as it may have seemed, music was never a "job" to her. She'd been foolish to believe she could give that up.

No amount of disappointment in the world could make her turn from singing, because it was the one thing that made her happy. In fact, it *owned* her. Ashanti announced her decision to pursue singing again. Although the family had mixed feelings, they were thrilled because they knew Ashanti had made the best choice.

She began working the gig circuit in some of New York's best clubs, including the famous China Club. Ashanti also began to feel confident about her impressive entertainment background in which she had gained many contacts.

Important people in the music industry were impressed by Ashanti's elegant and sophisticated performances, and it did not take long before the chairman of AJM Records, Mario L. Baeza, requested to talk business with her. Baeza then introduced Ashanti to big shot music producer Irving Lorenzo (better known as Irv Gotti) in 2001.

The meeting with Irv meant the world to Ashanti, but to Irv, it was just a repaid favor—he had no intentions of signing Ashanti. Further, he was not thoroughly impressed with Ashanti's demo tapes and felt that his streetwise rap label, Murder Inc., had no room for a supple singer.

He suggested that Ashanti look somewhere else for a contract. Yet, Ashanti was not going to be rejected or disappointed that easily the third time around. She did her best to expose herself to Irv, explaining her plans as a singer and her determination to succeed.

Ashanti eventually wore Irv down, and though he made her no promises, he told her to "come around". Little did he know, this invitation provided Ashanti with the time she needed to be able to sway Irv into seeing what a great addition she would be to his label.

Track 8: "Unfoolish"

Ashanti's mother was not thrilled about her choice to attempt to become an artist on the Murder Inc. label. Tina neither felt that the gangsta rap producer was the best fit for her daughter, nor that her potential label mates (many whom had committed crimes or done time) were the best people for her to surround herself with. Ashanti assured her mother that she was overreacting.

They second-guessed themselves as they approached the studio. The building resembled a run-down garage, with rusted doors, graffiti, and overgrown, patchy grass. To make matters worse,

the studio was called "The Crackhouse". It was unlike any studio Ashanti had ever been to, and Irv was unlike any producer Ashanti had ever met.

Furthermore, the label was different than any other label she had been involved with, because her potential label mates were all men. The studio housed more men than she had ever seen in one place at the same time. It was then that she understood that Irv was testing her strength. She understood immediately that being nervous or shy in this intimidating setting would not win her the recording contract she so badly desired.

Ashanti studied the artists and learned their personalities. She knew who had a sense of humor and who never smiled. Similarly, the rappers concentrated on Ashanti, and in time became comfortable with having her around. Like the boys she used to race against in her childhood, once she gained their respect, she was ready to learn from them. They taught her about the streets, and she began to think of Murder Inc. as her family.

Track 9: "Focus"

Irv's brother, Chris, agreed to allow Ashanti to exhibit her talents…but on the sidelines. Again, she had to prove herself to Murder Inc.; but, she was grateful for the opportunity and took on the challenge. Ashanti was to sing hooks and write for other artists. Her first assignment was to work with the late rapper Big Pun on his single "How We Roll".

Ashanti became extremely assertive in her quest to stardom, and whenever there was an opportunity for her to showcase her talent as a writer or singer, she made sure that her name was on the list. Thoroughly impressed with her determination, Irv finally signed Ashanti. At age twenty, Ashanti had landed her third recording contract.

By signing Ashanti, Irv had broadened his label's concept. In fact, she was just the element he needed. He had been disappointed in 1999 when Ja Rule's album had not done as well as he anticipated. He saw Ashanti as the missing ingredient that he needed to make his top artist's next album reach a level of success that he would be satisfied with.

Ashanti gladly lent her compelling vocals to Ja Rule's "Always On Time". The song became the most sold Def Jam single ever. Another Top 10 hit fell into Ashanti's lap when she sang the hook to Fat Joe's "What's Luv?" It would not be long until Ashanti would have the chance to shine on her own project.

Ashanti released "Foolish" in March 2002. She used the background from the Notorious B.I.G.'s "One More Chance" to help propel the single to a ten-week stint on the Billboard R&B/ Hip-Hop charts. The song became her most sold single, and was played on every radio station around the country. It gave competition to songs like Michael Jackson's "Thriller", which was at one time the most played song in history.

Within three weeks of its debut, "Foolish" surpassed five thousand spins on the radio and Ashanti became R&B's most talked about new artist.

♪rack 10: "♫iving ♫y ♫ife"

Irv and Ashanti had different views on the promotion of the *Ashanti* album. Ashanti thought it important to have positive feedback from the media and her fans. She felt that this would be reward enough for all of her years of hard work. Irv on the other hand, was thinking financially, and was most concerned who would be the best audience to market to. He realized Ashanti was not the everyday R&B singer, and he felt her album should be perceived in the same light. Luckily, each party was open to the other's opinion, and their marketing scheme proved to be quite successful.

It quickly became clear to audiences that Ashanti was no one's carbon copy. The *Ashanti* album was a fantastic fusion of R&B and hip-hop, and Irv thought that her first video should also be a product of successful fusion. Irv combined Ashanti's sweet voice and physical beauty with gritty gangster life as he fashioned the "Foolish" video after the film *Goodfellas*. The video

served as a visual translation of Ashanti joining Murder Inc. and was also an effort to gain men's interest in her music.

Ashanti became Murder Inc.'s tool to appeal to both sexes. She also became the label's most valuable chart-stopper.

Ashanti's debut album was finally released in April 2002 after years of hard work and disappointing record deals. *Ashanti* easily claimed the top spot on the Billboard R&B/Hip-Hop album chart by selling a whopping 500,000 copies within the first week. Veteran Celine Dion's latest album and newcomer Tweet's debut could not compete. Irv Gotti was speechless.

Tweet's album impressively sold 195,000 copies during its release week, but this figure was dwarfed by Ashanti's sales. The media attempted to create a rivalry between the two new R&B singers, however, they were both uninterested in playing into the drama. Tweet made her statement to the media by buying *Ashanti*, while Ashanti revealed that she was one of Tweet's avid fans. Ashanti believed in supporting positive black people in all walks of life.

Ashanti had huge crossover appeal and had accumulated a very diverse fan base. Some of her biggest fans were her fellow musicians who constantly requested that she write hits for them. Jennifer Lopez was one lucky recipient when Ashanti presented her with the chart topping "Ain't it Funny" remix.

All the while, the writing that she had done on her debut album continued to flourish. The album made history when it tied the Beatles' record of having three song entries all within the top ten on the Billboard 100 list at the same time. She was only the second musician to accomplish this record, and the first woman.

𝒯rack 11: "𝒰 Say, 𝒯 Say"

Although Ashanti had easily become the princess of Murder Inc. from the moment she set foot in the studio, the label felt that she needed a more encompassing title, and labeled her the "Princess of Hip-Hop and R&B". Audiences were steamed. They felt she hadn't the right to claim such a title. After all, she was new to superstardom, and such long-lasting, grandiose titles are usually reserved for record- and ground-breaking veterans. Aretha Franklin, Michael Jackson, James Brown, and Mary J. Blige are all artists who have earned their titles through multiple albums and years upon years of success. Many felt that Ashanti had not earned a title of this caliber with only one album.

Due to a title that was given to her, Ashanti became one of the most ridiculed singers. Disapproval spread amongst the media and critics who already questioned Ashanti's talent and songwriting ability, causing her album to suffer a sudden slew of negativity.

Some people began to discredit her amazing record sales by accusing Murder Inc. of buying a large quantity of them, while others said it was due to a rebate that the label offered on the album, which substantially pushed down its price. Still others said that her success was due to superstar guests like the Notorious B.I.G. and Ja Rule. The skepticism led to vicious crusades against Ashanti when it was announced that she was set to get the 2002 Soul Train "Aretha Franklin Entertainer of the Year Award".

Ashanti tried her best to shrug off the sudden barrage of negativity she was facing and continued to promote her album. She released "Down 4 U" featuring Ja Rule from the *Irv Gotti Presents The Inc.* album, and shortly after, released "Happy" from her own album. She was presented with a "Teen Choice Award", and began to work on the "Happy" video— tributed to and filmed in her hometown of Glen Cove, with Ja Rule.

The bond that Ja Rule and Ashanti had formed and the numerous songs they had performed together triggered a new set of rumors into circulation. The public was convinced that they were a couple, but the duo claimed that they simply enjoyed working together because they understood each other's sound.

Although Ashanti was singing about how "Happy" she was, reality was causing her to experience a much different emotion. A member of the public had become so outraged that Ashanti was chosen to receive the "Aretha Franklin Lady of

Soul Award"—an award recognizing the most talented overall performer of the year—that he began an on-line petition in hopes of making Soul Train choose a candidate that would cause less of a stir. The petition received a staggering 25,000 signatures, but Soul Train did not budge. The awards show not only strongly felt that Ashanti *was* deserving of the award, but also that she was *the* most deserving candidate for the award.

Ashanti and Murder Inc. as a whole stayed quiet about the situation. They all realized that the best defense would be proof that Ashanti deserved the award. She had her chance to do so when she opened the Soul Train Awards. Her performance was outstanding, and when she received the controversial award, she received a standing ovation. She was also nominated for four other awards that evening, and walked away with a trophy for "Best New Solo Artist".

"Happy" eased into the top ten, and Ashanti supported one of her favorite philanthropies, the American Cancer Society, at its 18th Annual Dream ball in New York.

The buzz about the petition dissolved, yet Ashanti's hardships did not disintegrate quite as easily.

Track 12: "Shany's World"

Ashanti began to do what it seems all celebrities do once they achieve a certain level of fame: find other outlets to exploit their talent. She decided to share her poetry with the world and released *Foolish/Unfoolish: Reflections on Love*, a compilation of her emotions and thoughts on past relationships. She lent her voice to *The Proud Family* cartoon, and enlisted in the lead role of a remake of the movie *Sparkle* with pal Ja Rule.

She stayed equally busy with appearances, attending the Mobo awards in London, performing at the Neil Bogart's Tour for a

Cure, and making a public announcement for World AIDS Day. She was cast as Dionne Warwick in NBC's *American Dreams*, was named Best R&B Artist in *Rolling Stone* magazine, and held the top spot at the 2002 Billboard Music Awards winning eight awards. The princess even somehow found time to perform at the 34th Street holiday concert in Madison Square Garden. Enhancing her satisfaction in the entertainment world, *Ashanti* went triple platinum.

Irv was the first producer who followed through with his promise and made Ashanti's dreams come true, and in return, Ashanti turned his company into a household name. Along with releasing her next track "Baby" from her own album, she was featured on Ja Rule's "Mesmerize", and various songs from *Irv Gotti Presents… The Remixes*. It seemed that anything that Ashanti influenced, whether it be through vocals or song writing, was destined to be a success.

Ashanti switched to acting again during February when she had a cameo on *Buffy the Vampire Slayer*. She went on to win her first Grammy for Best Contemporary R&B Album for *Ashanti*. Though she only achieved success through hard work, it seemed that once she crossed the threshold, acclaim and opportunity fell directly into her lap.

Track 13: "The Story of 2"

Ashanti was the new golden girl. Not only had she been nominated for the industry's top awards *and* won them, she had grown to understand the industry and become an apt businesswoman. Although deeply involved in numerous charity performances and an intense book tour schedule, Ashanti decided it was time to make a second album.

She believed that releasing a follow-up album would quiet the people who were doubtful about her talent and would allow Ashanti to truly demonstrate her abilities. She was ready for the next chapter in her craft and her life, and saw that it only made sense to name her next album *Chapter 2*.

On top of her frequent studio sessions that many times lasted until five in the morning, Ashanti continued to accept awards and perform. She was nominated for a NAACP Image Award, and won for Outstanding New Artist. In addition, she continued her charitable work by arranging a concert that was free for the soldiers who fought the "War on Terrorism" and their families.

She found it very difficult to focus on her new album while still performing past hits. She also began to experience conflicts with Irv over the production of *Chapter 2*.

Ashanti was a perfectionist who would rewrite her music an uncountable amount of times until she felt it was perfect; Irv was a businessman who found many of the revisions unnecessary.

Irv became very frustrated because he felt that as a producer, his opinion should be heeded. It was at this point that he realized that what Ashanti was doing was creating art, and that for the sake of art, it is necessary that the artist make the final decision. He gave her space, but was still worried that she would never be completely satisfied with the finished product.

Ashanti finally felt that she was ready to release her first single from her sophomore album, "Rock Wit U (Awww Baby)". Irv was very happy with the finished product and thankful that he had decided to give the artist the space she needed to create. The tables had turned, and Ashanti now held the role of the teacher—showing Irv fresh ways to make songs, and teaching him more about R&B music and hit records than he expected.

Ashanti was suddenly hit with the responsibility of carrying the entire Murder Inc. label as Ja Rule decided to take an unexpected vacation. She greeted the task with maturity and decided to make her maturity visible in her image as well. Ashanti established a more adult style of dress and warmed her hair and make-up with earth tones. She transformed from the young princess of R&B into a sexy and sophisticated woman.

Her growth as a singer and woman caught Mariah Carey's eye, and Ashanti signed on to be the perfect opening act for Mariah's 2003 tour.

Track 14: "Fight"

The release of *Chapter* 2 posed a new threat; Ashanti was no longer a rookie in the business, and her competition had changed. Beyoncé had decided to release a solo album during a brief hiatus from Destiny's Child, as well as both Mya and Monica. Each of these women had grown and reinvented themselves since the time they first entered the music industry scene, and targeted the same fans as Ashanti did. The charts became a battleground.

The biggest clash Ashanti faced was against Beyoncé. The ladies were compared to each other from appeal and dancing style to talent. They were also equally criticized; the public critiqued Beyoncé's singing and flashy awards show performances, while they harped on Ashanti's new hair color and how much she exposed her body this time around.

Ashanti did not know what to expect with the release of *Chapter 2*, but she stood behind her album confidently. She was happy alone with the satisfaction she felt from releasing a project over which she had control.

Chapter 2 was not the only thing Ashanti had control over; she had also gained control of her image and emotions. This album allowed Ashanti to flaunt her sex appeal and had forced her to develop a backbone for public rejection. Ashanti had to stand on her own and bring out the best of her abilities; this was heightened by the fact that Ja Rule was not anywhere to be found on the release.

Although popular opinion of *Chapter 2* greatly varied as it was voted both Best and Worst album of 2003, there was no disputing that it was a favorite among Ashanti fans. The album sold more than 320,000 copies in its first week and became number one on the Billboard 200 LP and R&B and Hip-Hop charts. More notably, it temporarily ended her musical battle with Beyoncé as she knocked her rival's album *Dangerously in Love* from the top chart positions.

Track 15: "Rain On Me"

Ashanti now had *two* number one albums to add to her resumé. Both Beyoncé and Monica expressed interest in touring with her.

She showed her maturity by releasing "Rain On Me" as her second single. She found it very important to bring women's issues to the forefront—even those that happened behind closed doors such as domestic violence. The release received praise, and the remix received a Grammy nomination.

She rounded out her days of album promoting with photo shoots, interviews, and signing on for various roles in films and musicals. She found it hard to give song writing and recording her full attention with such a strenuous schedule, but it would be the issues within her record label that caused the most stress on Ashanti's upcoming days.

Murder Inc.'s name had come back to haunt the label. Members of the organization had been accused of playing roles in various criminal activities, and the label's infatuation with the word "murder" caused the public to believe the allegations were true. Murder Inc.'s future had been threatened, and Ashanti's career was suddenly in jeopardy.

Ashanti became the spokesperson for her label. The sexy R&B singer proved that the label was not about crime, but instead about entertainment. She defended the label explaining that the word "murder" had been misinterpreted—it meant that their label "murdered" the competition. It was simply a metaphor and was not to be taken literally.

Ashanti soon found that the best way to defend her company was not with words, but instead by example. She continued involving herself in the philanthropic efforts that always brought her pleasure. The star became active in both the Amelia Quinn Outreach Program and The Rock to Vote Program, which sought to bring children in unfortunate areas and situations closer to entertainers while also teaching the importance of education.

She also had an opportunity to show the public the real side of her life in VH-1's "Driven" and MTV's "Diary". Each of these shows presented the public with an occasion to see Ashanti in her natural element, without the glitz and glamour of celebrity. In addition, Ashanti opted to release a Christmas album in hopes of benefiting her fans as well as Murder Inc.'s dwindling presence.

It was at this time that Murder Inc. decided that it was in the company's best interest to change the label's name to The Inc. Irv finally realized that the label's name had contributed to the organization's problems and also that the name limited the company's capabilities. It was completely inappropriate to release a Christmas album under the title "Murder Inc.", and Ashanti had been passed up for several endorsement opportunities because of the label's name.

There is speculation that Ashanti threatened to leave the label if the name was not changed. She had seen the damage that it had caused her own career and the image of the label at large. Perhaps Irv not only realized that Ashanti's points were valid, but also that she was a great asset to the company—an asset that his suffering company could not afford to lose. Regardless of the reasons for the name change, it was a step in the positive direction and benefited all parties involved.

Track 16: "Wonderful"

Although troubles continued to ferment at The Inc., Ashanti's career continued to be successful. She discovered another arena of competition in which she and Beyoncé were to face off as the two battled for ownership of a 2003 MTV Music Award and for the "Best Contemporary R&B Album", "Best R&B Album", and "Best Female R&B Performance" at the 2004 Grammy Awards. The dominating success that Ashanti had experienced during record release was reversed, as Beyoncé was the evening's biggest winner. Ashanti graciously applauded her biggest rival.

Although she had lost at the Grammy's, Ashanti had a lot to be happy about. She had landed a role in 2005's *Coach Carter* starring one of Hollywood's biggest African-American stars, Samuel L. Jackson. Ashton Kutcher even focused on her during an episode of his show "Punk'd", a show in which he playfully torments top celebrities. She had truly become a household name.

Ashanti did not take long to start working on her fourth album *Concrete Rose* which debuted at number seven, selling thousands of copies in its first week. She released "Only You", which debuted at number one, as the album's first single. Again she demonstrated her bond with Ja Rule as she sang on his song "Wonderful" along with R. Kelly. Ashanti also discovered that she had an interest in following Madonna's footsteps and hopes to pen a children's book, or a "behind the scenes" book in the near future.

Paul Bryant, a DJ at New York's Z100, sums up Ashanti's ongoing success by saying, "She appeals to an urban audience and a pop audience. She doesn't lean one way or another. She's edgy but not too edgy. It's really good for an artist to be in the middle because it's how you sell records." She had passed on this important "middle-of-the-road" lesson to her producer, Irv, as he opted to change his label's name, and also as he decided to sign on other winning R&B prospects. Ashanti had both directly and indirectly influenced The Inc. to regain its popularity and success.

In spite of all of the rugged and street-wise men that make up The Inc., it is the gentle presence of Ashanti that truly provides strength to the label. Ashanti is often exploited by other artists as a singer/song-writer in order to enrich scenarios and ensure a track's success. She is the component that completes many situations, rounding out any rough edges with her soft femininity.

Ashanti has struggled to achieve her success, and though many times she may have felt lost or hopeless, she always depended on her heart to steer her in the correct direction. She has strengthened her self-esteem by staying true to herself and what she finds important despite the opinions of others. Ashanti has followed the song in her heart, and translated it into the song of her life.

Beyoncé

Beyoncé Knowles

Interlude

Beyoncé's confidence in music came long before she had gained any acclaim or won any awards. The star who was born on September 4, 1981, performed in her first talent show at age seven and received a standing ovation for her rendition of "Imagine". Before the talent show ended, Beyoncé told her mother that she wanted to "get [her] trophy, get [her] money, and go, because [she was] hungry". Her mother attempted to contain her ego by explaining that the contest was over, and they did not yet know who was actually going to win the event; however, it was not long before Beyoncé's confidence was proven valid, as she was announced as the first place winner.

Years later, after achieving phenomenal international success with the group Destiny's Child, Beyoncé decided that 2003 was the perfect time in her career to release a solo album. She gained immediate acclaim, because all of her mainstream exposure had made the release of *Dangerously in Love* highly anticipated. Audiences knew that the help she received from Missy Elliot, Jay Z, Sean Paul, Mario Winans, Big Boi, and Luther Vandross would only seal the potential success of the album.

They were right. Every song that was released from *Dangerously in Love* was an instant success. The album was more passionate, more mature, and more personal than anything she had ever done with Destiny's Child. "Me, Myself, and I", "Baby Boy" and "Naughty Girl" achieved the same extreme and immediate success that "Crazy in Love" had, causing the album to reach multi-platinum status. It only made sense when she embarked on her first sold-out tour as a solo artist with co-headliners Missy Elliot and Alicia Keys.

Critics loved *Dangerously in Love* as much as her fans did. Beyoncé found herself overwhelmed as she was the biggest winner at MTV Music Awards, BET Awards, and even the Grammy Awards, where she tied the record set by Lauryn Hill in 1999 by taking home five awards.

Beyoncé Knowles

Destiny's Child

Destiny's Child

Unlike most other musicians, Destiny's Child's rise to fame was a beautifully crafted fairytale about four young women who were blessed with the "fairest voices in all the land". Every day these women worked diligently and waited patiently to be discovered by their Prince Charming: the music industry. This is not to say that the four Houston girls traveled the road to fame without disappointments and set backs; but instead, that once their "Knight in Shining Armor" stumbled upon them that fateful day in 1997, they knew that all of their dreams would come true and that they were destined to live happily-ever-after.

Track 1: "Show Me The Way"

The group took its first steps on the pathway to its destiny when Girl's Tyme, a group founded by later Destiny's Child co-manager, Andretta Tillman, was founded in 1991. Thirty girls auditioned for a position, but only six were chosen—three of whom were Beyoncé Knowles, Kelendria "Kelly" Rowland, and LaTavia Roberson.

Though comprised of ten- and eleven-year-olds, Girl's Tyme attracted a lot of attention in Houston immediately. These young women provided an alternative to the male-heavy groups that ruled the music scene in the early

nineties. Their music combined R&B, Hip-Hop and pop, and the content of their songs ranged from boys to world unity.

The group's rigorous schedule of training six hours a day paid off as they received opportunities to perform at Houston's Black Expo, the Miss Black Houston Metroplex Pageant, the People's Workshop's Sammy Davis Jr. Awards, and opened for popular rapper Yo-Yo. They were featured in *Crossroads* TV magazine, and praised in the *Houston Chronicle*. Reportedly, Prince expressed interest twice in signing the girl's group to his record label.

However, the group thought that their biggest recognition materialized when they were presented with an opportunity to perform on Star Search, the talent show that had launched the careers of many prominent entertainers. When they did not win, they were devastated.

After the show, changes started to take place in the group. Three members left, leaving only Beyoncé, Kelly, and LaTavia. LeToya Luckett joined the three, and Matthew Knowles, Beyoncé's father, signed on as co-manager. Lastly, the group

changed its name to "Destiny's Child," a phrase Beyoncé's mom, Tina, happened upon while reading the Bible.

Despite the girls' demoralizing loss on *Star Search*, Matthew was very pleased with the girls' progress. He wanted to take the girls from city-wide stardom to world-wide stardom, and took the task so seriously that he resigned from his job as a neurological sales specialist to devote all off his time to the group. Tina Knowles brought her hair care specialties and fashion capabilities to the table, as she became Destiny's Child's official stylist.

Year after year, the quartet traveled from all corners of Houston to rehearse. They enlisted in singing and dance lessons to harness their God-given talents. They did all of this while willingly sacrificing much of the fun and freedom that are found in childhood. It seemed much easier to make these sacrifices within a group than it would have if they were pursuing their journey alone.

During summer vacation, the girls would go to "Summer Camp". However, this summer experience was not about swimming and making s'mores. At Matthew Knowles' "Summer Camp", the girls' days were spent jogging three miles each day, followed by eight hours of practice—including aerobics and drills.

By the time the young women reached high school, they had been training so meticulously over the years, that achieving their musical goals was their primary focus. They did not fall prey to the typical teenage girl distractions such as partying and boys, and in fact, became so involved with their training that they found it necessary to enlist tutors to help their studies as well as be partially home-schooled.

Although everyone believed in and supported the girls' dream, LaTavia's mother, Cheryl Mitchell, did have concerns. She did not want to discourage her daughter, but she did want her to be realistic and realize that regardless of all of her hard work, "her dream [might] not be realized." The girls heeded her advice, becoming maturely realistic, but they never lost hope in their dream. Cheryl soon saw that her apprehension was in vain.

Track 2: "So Good"

Late one summer day in 1997, the casually dressed quartet was hanging out in the studio. They really had no legitimate reason for being there, as they were not recording or taking part in a publicity shoot. The girls chatted and giggled while Matthew spoke to a visitor, and it wasn't long before Matthew asked the girls to sing for the guest. Despite the unexpectedness of the request, the girls gave a flawless acapella performance that stunned the man. On this auspicious day, the quartet had impressed the right person: he was a writer for a local newspaper.

He wrote a highly complimentary article about the girls referring to them as a "quartet of angels" and commenting that their sound was an "aural collage so beautiful, it could hardly have come from four teenagers". He warned the world that these teens were going to "set the Rhythm-and-Blues industry on its ear in the next few months".

This beautifully worded yet blunt article stimulated the curiosity of many associated with the music industry, including Columbia Records.

Destiny's Child signed with Columbia Records, and before they had even released a single song, they had sparked the interest of some of the most popular and talented producers. Their album had a culmination of tastes, as they worked with producers from every corner of the US: Dwayne Wiggins of Tony, Toni, Tone, Wyclef, Master P, and Jermaine Dupri. Aside from producing chart-topping hits, all of these men had proven that they possessed the ability to spot a potential star throughout their careers; they all saw that unique quality within Destiny's Child.

Evidently, Columbia also saw this quality in the group, and opted to add their song "Killing Time" to the *Men In Black* soundtrack before the public even knew who they were. In a day where movie soundtracks are mostly sold due to an all-star line up, relying on an unknown group was a leap of faith and a vote of confidence.

Destiny's Child would not remain unknown long, as they released their first single "No, No, No" to radio airplay. Yet, it was label mate Wyclef's production of the remix of the song that truly shot the group to fame, as the song went platinum shortly after its release. Audiences became interested in what else the quartet had to offer, and February's release of *Destiny's Child* became an instant chart climber.

Although pleased with the positive response and level of talent these young ladies possessed, Columbia was especially impressed with a trait that they had *learned* along the way. Though young, these women had wisely listened to their mentors, such as R&B group SWV, and had gained priceless knowledge about the music industry. One of the most important lessons they had learned from their musical mentors as well as their parents was the importance of maintaining a classy image. For this, Columbia did not feel that they had to worry about how the girls would conduct themselves during interviews or whether they could handle the stress that comes along with fame.

Unfortunately, their original musical mentor and manager, Andretta Tillman, passed away just as the girls were first beginning to experience success in 1997. The group was heartbroken and collectively decided to honor their friend by dedicating their song, "My Time has Come" to her memory.

Their sadness was caressed by the success their album was achieving; they knew that Andretta would have been eternally pleased that "No, No, No" had gone multi-platinum and was number one on Billboard Top Albums chart and *Destiny's Child* had sold nearly 500,000 copies.

Suddenly, the girls found their days more demanding than any day at "Summer Camp" had been. There schedule was filled with promotional and tour dates throughout both the US and Europe. They went on tour with Boys II Men and won three of four coveted Soul Train Lady of Soul Awards, including "Best Single", "Best Album", and "Best New Artists". Though Destiny's Child felt they were at the peak of their fame, the group's momentum began to grow.

Track 3: "Lose My Breath"

Destiny's Child did not take a break, as most artists do, after experiencing such widespread recognition for a debut album. Instead, the women used the success of *Destiny's Child,* as an inspiration to hurry back to the studio. This time around, they again received help from Dwayne Wiggins, as well as Missy Elliot and She'kspere. The first album took 2½ years to release; but, *The Writing's on the Wall* would only take 2½ months. More importantly than the drastically shortened production time, the girls were allowed more creative input on their second album.

Through their surmounting success, Destiny's Child wanted to be sure that they were recognized for the right reasons. While being attractive definitely had countless advantages, the group realized the blessing forced them to work harder to make people see their artistic abilities. Although physically beautiful and constantly displaying their perfect, shapely figures in sexy clothing, they found it more important that fans drool over their talent. The girls felt that the best way to ensure this outcome was to remain thoroughly involved in each step of their music.

The members of Destiny's Child were given the chance to write and produce almost all of the tracks on their sophomore album. They proved that they were worthy of the opportunity

when their first track from *The Writing's on the Wall*, "Bills, Bills Bills" reached number one on pop charts.

With this song, Destiny's Child became the group that, although producing danceable music, served as spokeswomen for female motivation. In many of their songs, they staked their independence or called for all women to demand more respect from their men. They warned deceitful men to straighten their priorities. Women throughout the world welcomed the empowerment while also being able to dance to the music. The message was strong, but the music was not heavy or depressing.

The continued preaching their messages to men and women alike with the releases of "Bug A Boo", "Say My Name", and "Jumpin Jumpin," which also reached top ten and became a number one hit on the *Billboard* Hot 100.

Matthew Knowles was a savvy business man and knew the importance of endorsements and promotions. He organized major tours for Destiny's Child and arranged for the members to sign a contract with Soft & Beautiful Botanicals hair care products. This allowed the group to promote itself while endorsing the products on television, radio, and billboards. To ensure that no potential audience was missed, Matthew distributed promotional CD packages containing samples of the hair care products to salons. Destiny's Child was everywhere.

Track 4: "Illusions"

Suddenly, at the pinnacle of the Destiny's Child's success, the group announced that it was breaking up. The announcement reached shocked fans just days before the Grammy Awards, where the group was nominated for "Best R&B Song" and "Best R&B Performance by a Duo or Group".

To this day, no one but the group knows the true reason that LeToya and LaTavia decided to leave their Grammy-nominated group after almost ten years of performing together. There was speculation that the two wanted to attend college and pursue other opportunities. Others were sure that the split occurred as a result that the two were not receiving their fair share of the group's earnings. LeToya and LaTavia claimed the rift was caused because they wanted to replace their manager, whom they felt showed favoritism to certain members. It was no secret that his daughter, Beyoncé, was the lead singer, and her sidekick, Kelly, had been raised as his daughter. Beyoncé, Kelly, and manager Matthew, felt that the girls attempted to have all of their demands met by exploiting a vulnerable situation at a crucial time: it was the crux of the group's true career success as they had just released their sophomore album, been nominated for Grammy Awards, and begun to develop their newest video, "Say My Name". Although there were various opinions about the deconstruction of the group, the public had come to a consensus, and time would only prove, that LeToya and LaTavia had made a grave mistake.

The remaining components of Destiny's Child floundered around for a couple of weeks trying to determine the future of the group. They did not know whether it was best for them to reconcile with their irate members, search for replacement members, or continue as a duo. Beyoncé was on the verge of a nervous breakdown and stayed in her bed for two weeks. Kelly also tried to deal with her disappointments and frustrations. In the end, the girls found comfort in prayer, and relying on their Christian faith to lead them in the right direction. During this time, which they called "Prayer Week", the two remaining members forged a tighter bond, and found that the best solution to their problem would be to find two new members to make Destiny's Child a quartet again.

Track 5: "Now That She's Gone"

Destiny's Child needed two new members that could not only sing and dance, but who also had the look, grace, and style that fit the image that the successful group had already established. The two people that seemed to fit these criteria the best were Michelle Williams, from Rockford, Illinois, and Farrah Franklin from Los Angeles.

Adding to Destiny's Child's fairytale story, these two performers were approached with a perfectly fitting glass slipper. Both of these elegant women had established an impressionable

background in music: Michelle was a background singer for R&B artist, Monica, and Farrah had already created a bond with Destiny's Child members as she danced in their "Bills, Bills, Bills" video.

If Destiny's Child's former members had hoped to halt the group's success by leaving at such a crucial instant, they had not succeeded. The new team practiced their routines for hours each day, and shined at their various performances and appearances. The more the girls performed together, the more comfortable they became with one another. They shot the "Say My Name" video and created an imaginative video that was worthy of the songs popularity. Despite the confusing changes the group underwent, the video also became one of MTV's most popular selections.

The group performed at the 2000 NBA All-Star Game, as well as at the Soul Train Awards. Michelle found that fans had immediately accepted the new members, and expressed her delight when she said, "It was great! People were already screaming my name, which felt good". Although the group seemed to be prospering without any additional drama from

former members, media, or fans, everyone waited on the edge of their seats to see what would occur at the Grammy Awards that year.

The group had been nominated for two Grammy Awards for the ceremony's 42nd year. For this, it seemed only fitting that "Destiny's Child", which was now comprised of two new members, would accept any awards that night. Contrarily, it also seemed fitting that the two women who actually *recorded* the album's music, the two former members, deserved to accept any awards. The original members had not made amends; they neither arrived at the awards together, nor sat together.

The tension between the members was only thickened by the fact that no one knew what these girls would do if they won an award. Would all six women accept the award? Would they fight over the statue on stage? The public did not receive the drama they hoped for as the group did not win the opportunity to approach the stage.

With the confusion of the Grammy's brought to a close, the ties between the original members were also drawn to a conclusion. Beyoncé, Kelly, Farrah, and Michelle continued to identify themselves as "Destiny's Child" while LeToya and LaTavia had formed a new group which never really gained acclaim called "Angel".

Destiny's Child was dubbed the "Billboard Artist of the Year", and received an invite to perform at VH1's "Diva's Live". During this event, they were to share the stage with music veterans Diana Ross, Mariah Carey, and Faith Hill. They couldn't believe that they would be performing alongside some of the industry's best female performers, and used the opportunity to prove that they belonged there. The quartet danced on stage and promenaded through the audience while exhibiting their vocal skills on Diana Ross' "Upside Down".

In the six months following the break-up, the singers sold more records and performed more than they had in the six months prior to the break-up; to date, *The Writing's on the Wall* has sold over ten million records worldwide. Some fans of the

original group pointed out that as far as record sales were concerned, the new members were enjoying the success that the original members' work had produced. It was at this time that Destiny's Child decided to release a new song that proved that the new members were deserving of any praise that the group received.

Track 6: "Bad Habit"

Recording "Independent Women Part 1" for the *Charlie's Angels* soundtrack was the first time that either Michelle or Farrah had been in a studio. They truly enjoyed the experience, and were happy to lend their vocals to another Beyoncé-written hit.

The quartet's schedule became more hectic than ever as their days became filled with activities from 7 a.m. to 2 a.m. They began a European tour in March of 2002, giving Michelle and Farrah their first opportunities to perform live as members of Destiny's Child. Once completing the tour, the young women flew back to New York to perform with Brian McKnight at Madison Square Garden.

However, their most fruitful live performance opportunity was when they were asked to tour with Christina Aguilera. Although Destiny's Child was Christina's opening act, their album *The Writing's on the Wall* was often outselling Aguilera's own self-titled album on a weekly basis. Touring with Aguilera allowed the group to broaden their core audience as many pop fans suddenly became interested in Destiny's Child's music after attending the concert.

Though it was clear that the group was on the path to success, the future of the group once again became hazy as they announced that Farrah would no longer be a member of the

group. The reasons for Farrah's departure were just as cloudy as the reasons that LeToya and LaTavia left.

Destiny's Child said that Farrah told the group that she could not handle the hectic schedule and opted not to be a part of the group when she chose not to accompany them on their promotional tour in Australia. Farrah's story differed. She said that she had missed the promotional events because she was very ill, and under her doctor's orders to stay home. She said that Matthew Knowles became very controlling and verbally abusive when she informed him of the doctor's prescription. She also added that she too had witnessed the favoritism he showed for Beyoncé. The current rift proved that with Destiny's Child, the writing *was* on the wall, but it was left up to interpretation.

Farrah signed a deal with a different record label, and hoped to pursue a career in acting. Like the previous Destiny's Child former members before her, the public has not heard much about her since the day she left the group.

Track 7: "Survivor"

The group decided that is was in their best interest to continue on as trio. Audiences didn't seem to mind. Album sales of *The Writing's on the Wall* continued to rise as the concert with Christina continued to be a success.

In the fall of 2000, "Independent Women Part 1" finally hit airwaves and achieved immediate and long-lasting popularity as it held the Billboard's all-time record for "Most Airplay". Beyoncé was especially pleased with the success of the track, because she had not only written it, but also produced it.

Suddenly, with the extreme success of "Independent Women Part 1", the group found themselves being sued by LeToya and LaTavia. The women dropped the lawsuit against the group as they settled out of court for an undisclosed sum of money.

With the drama of past members stricken from their lives, the trio began working on their third album, and appropriately named it *Survivor*. Destiny's Child had survived despite all of down-falls and surprises that had been bestowed upon them. No one knew whether this song was dedicated to an ex-boy-friend or an ex-bandmember. As a further slap in the face to previous members who accused Matthew of favoritism, Beyoncé insured that her fellow members received bigger sing-ing roles on the new album, as she wrote and produced many of the songs.

The promotions continued to pour in as the girls signed on to represent AT&T and Candies. Beyoncé landed her own deal with L'Oreal. They also displayed the greatness of their own project, as *Survivor* debuted at number one on the Billboard

200 chart, and was certified as double platinum after only four weeks. The album went on to sell over nine million copies around the world.

The album's hit songs "Survivor", "Bootylicious", and the remake of The BeeGees "Emotion", were played continuously on radio stations throughout the year. In fact, "Bootylicious" became so popular that it became a word in everyday speech; Webster's Dictionary solidified this fact by making the word an official entry. Today, Beyoncé has tired of the overuse of the word, as she is still described as "Bootylicious" years after the song's release.

The albums success earned them yet another trip to the Grammy Awards. The ladies performed and finally won the award, taking home the Grammy for "Best R&B Performance by a Duo or Group". They also won various AMA's, Soul Train, NAACP Image, Block Buster Entertainment, and Billboard Music Awards for *Survivor*.

The continuing success of the group left the young women reeling. Their music was popular among a varied crowd, and

their faces were well-known due to their numerous endorsements. However, the group found it continually important to prove that they were not only beautiful, but also talented, as individuals. Being a part of a group did not always give the girls the opportunity to display their individuality or show the world the extent of their talents. Destiny's Child had already proven that they were gifted despite their beauty, but they also wanted to ascertain that they were talented despite the support of other group members. Kelly, Michelle, and Beyoncé decided to spend the next few years working on their solo careers.

Track 8: "Independent Women"

Meet Michelle Williams:

Michelle Williams was born "Tenetira Michelle Williams", on July 23rd, 1980. She grew up very involved in her church, and unsurprisingly, discovered her talent and love for music while in church. Michelle was only seven when she awed her church's congregation with an inspiring solo rendition of "Blessed Assurance". By age twelve, she had earned the role of "choir director", as she was in charge of conducting the 500 members of the Martin Luther King Youth Choir.

She began her journey in music as a profession when she by chance learned of an opportunity to sing background vocals for R&B sensation, Monica. A friend, with whom she had been out of contact, randomly called her; during this conversation, Michelle discovered that the friend was a keyboardist for Monica. Michelle expressed an interest in singing background for the star, but was thoroughly surprised when her friend again called her a week later to inform her that Monica was holding auditions for background singers in Atlanta. Michelle immediately packed her bags for Atlanta.

Many girls auditioned for the part, but it was Michelle who landed the role. She moved to Atlanta and began to tour with Monica. When the tour ended, she moved back home to Rockford, Illinois expecting to restart her normal life; however, her life would be forever changed as she received a phone call and an offer from Destiny's Child.

Although thoroughly appreciative of the successes she had achieved since joining Destiny's Child, she was equally excited about having the opportunity to pursue a solo career. Her dedication to the church had not diminished as she had grown or achieved stardom, and she desperately wanted to release a gospel album.

Her desires were fulfilled in April 2002, when her contemporary gospel collection, "Heart to Yours" was released. The album reached number one on the Top Gospel Albums chart, and inspired her to release a second album, "Do You Know" in January, 2004. The second album brought Michelle similar success, as it reached number three on the Top Gospel Album chart, and number two on the Top Christian Album chart.

She also pursued her love for the theater when she earned the lead role in Broadway's Aida, in November 2003. The role was originally filled by singer Toni Braxton, but Toni decided that she wanted to devote more time to her family. Michelle was chosen to replace her, and she received rave reviews for her portrayal of "Aida".

Know Kelly Rowland

Kelly was the second member to gain her individuality, and pursue projects that would truly soothe her soul. Kelly's split from Beyoncé would be more dramatic than many would think because the two had grown up together, literally.

Kelly was born on February 11, 1981 and was raised by her mother Doris. Doris fell on hard times in the early nineties, and she and Kelly moved into the Knowles' home in order to surround themselves with a more stable environment. From this moment, Kelly's family rapidly grew, as she now had three parents and had gained two sisters. Luckily, her family had the same inclination towards music that she had.

Kelly's interest in music began at age four when she sang in church; later, she sacrificed much of her childhood for the further pursuit of music.

Kelly had first performed music without her group members when she was featured on R&B singer Avant's, "Separated" remix in 2000, which rose to top five on the charts. She again used the formula of combining her skills with a sexy musician when she and rapper Nelly released the "Dilemma". The hit was number one on the Billboard charts for several weeks, and went on to win the Grammy for "Best Rap/Sung Collaboration". There was also talk that she and Nelly continued their relationship off screen.

Her album, *Simply Deep*, had more of a pop feel than her material with Destiny's Child, and became an international success. The album was especially popular in England, where it was

number one on many of the UK's charts. In the US, the album also experienced popularity, as it peaked at number three on the Billboard Top Hip-Hop/R&B chart.

Hanging around Beyoncé's movie sets caused Kelly to gain an interest in trying her own hand at acting. She was given her first opportunity when she earned a role in the 2003's thriller, *Freddy vs. Jason*. Enjoying her experience, she looks forward to continue acting in the future.

However, what excites Kelly the most is her upcoming marriage to professional football player, Roy Williams, of the Dallas Cowboys. After dating for six months, Roy proposed to her in May 2004. Of course, Kelly asked Beyoncé to be one of her bridesmaids during the 2005 wedding.

Become Re-Acquainted with Beyoncé Knowles

Beyoncé used her time away from her group members to first chase another one of her loves: acting. In 2001, she pounced on the opportunity to demonstrate her acting skills when she play the lead role in MTV's *Carmen: A Hip-Hopera*—a modern day remake of the critically acclaimed *Carmen*—beside sexy Mekhi Pfifer.

She took advantage of the opportunity to be featured on the big screen when she played Mike Myer's leading lady in the third installment of the Austin Powers movies, *Goldmember*. Beyoncé further exhibited her talents on the soundtrack to the film with "Work it Out". The single, released not long after the 2002 release of the film, was a hit reminiscent of the soul and funk of the seventies.

She again played the leading lady in 2003's, *The Fighting Temptations,* costarring Cuba Gooding Jr., and again lent her vocal talents to the film's soundtrack on "I Know". The movie's plot was centered on music and Beyoncé's musical desires were once again rekindled.

She exploded back on the music scene with her featured spot on Jay Z's "Bonnie and Clyde '03". The song raced to the top of the charts and made the number one position its home for several weeks.

Jay Z returned the favor with his featured spot on "Crazy in Love", the first release from her debut solo album, which also became very comfortable in the number one position. The professional success that the duo experienced leaked into their personal lives, as Jay Z and Beyoncé have been inseparable ever since. *It is rumored that Beyoncé herself, like Kelly, is also to be married by the end of 2005.*

Aside from her numerous music awards, Beyoncé continued to set records as she was awarded a contract from Tommy Hilfiger to market her own fragrance, *True Star.* Joining superstars Jennifer Lopez, Britney Spears, and Jessica Simpson, Beyoncé was the first African-American woman to have her own fragrance.

She also spent time promoting Pepsi and L'Oreal products before she realized she would like to also express her creativity within her own business. She and her mother, Tina, decided to follow in the footsteps of so many musicians before her, and created a clothing line. House of Dereon, named for her seam-stress grandmother, Agnes Dereon, will first market children's clothing, and in time, add adult clothing to its lineup. The clothing line, which is produced by the Knowles' family company, Beyond Productions, will be distributed in 2005.

Remarkably, her ambitions do not end there. Prior to the release of her solo debut, Beyoncé said that she aspired to win an Oscar and a Grammy by the time she was 31. Perhaps her role as the leading lady opposite Steve Martin in the prequel to "The Pink Panther" will further her in her journey of achieving the other half of her goal. The film is due in theaters mid 2005.

Ꞇrack 9: "ꟻree"

Although each member had achieved varying degrees of success during her time apart from the group, they each truly missed the dynamic that the group provided. Being away from each other allowed the girls to discover an appreciation for what each member artistically brought to the group. Somehow, the time the women had spent as soloists thickened their bond as a group, and they were excited to evoke that feeling in their new album.

The trio put themselves on a strict three week schedule of recording—even less time than they allowed themselves for *The Writings on the Wall*. With the new album, they wanted to create music that was "timeless and set a new standard"; and due to their growth as individuals, they were able to achieve that.

Destiny Fulfilled was an album that evoked more emotion than any other Destiny's Child album had. Beyoncé supported this by saying, "You hear our vulnerability. We've always had strong songs that encouraged women and you still hear that this time, but you will also hear our weaknesses: the crying, the laughter, the friendship." The album was again mostly written and produced by the members themselves; for this reason, *Destiny Fulfilled* served as a more intimate look into Destiny's Child's lives, thoughts, and desires.

After three years since releasing a song as a group, Destiny's Child made a loud entrance as it returned to the music scene with "Lose my Breath". The public loved them more than ever, and their single, as trend shows, immediately shot to the top of the charts. They did not waste time releasing "Soldier", featuring two of the dirty south's own soldiers, Lil' Wayne and TI. This song also leaped to the top of the charts. The album debuted at number two selling 500,000 records within its first week of release.

The acclaim continued for *Destiny Fulfilled* as "Lose my Breath" was nominated for a Grammy Award. Yet, although they have been nominated for countless awards, proven their talent within and without the support of a group and ventured into their souls' most craved endeavors, their destiny is anything but "fulfilled".

These women have an aura of longevity and they have consistently taken steps to make sure that neither the public nor they themselves become bored with their work. Destiny's Child keeps audiences guessing. Fans are often pleased with, yet importantly, still intrigued by the product in which Destiny's Child presents them. The public has planned to see these women's careers continue to blossom over the years, and looks forward to being entertained in the process.

Jennifer Lopez

Jennifer Lopez

Jennifer Lopez is one woman who can truly say she's done it all. If superstardom is a main goal in today's world, Jennifer Lopez is on *top* of the world. Jennifer has become one of the most popular and idolized actresses and singers, and over the past decade, we have learned that there is no limit to what she can do and nothing to stop her from achieving it. Jennifer has starred in hit movies, made award-winning albums, fine-tuned her love for dancing, guest starred on popular sitcoms, modeled for some of the world's top designers, and started her own company. As a result, it only makes sense that she has become the center of the media's nonstop attention.

The media has been relentless about capturing every detail of Jennifer's life. In addition to showcasing her upcoming releases or new endeavors, they also harshly criticize her relationships, personal life, and fuel any existing rumors. Instead of crumbling beneath the skepticism and negativity, Jennifer instead compiles it, and becomes stronger from it.

She is one of the most envied and mesmerizing entertainers the world has ever known and she has opened doors for many to follow in her footsteps. She has a universal appeal and has always shown pride in her heritage and upbringing. Most importantly for Jennifer, she has helped bring Hispanic culture to a high it's never experienced before. Once

Jennifer made it, others in her culture had the chance to be what they thought they never could. Through her achievements, Jennifer has showed all of us how blind the media and the world can be.

Although there have been many Hollywood trailblazers for the Hispanic culture in the past, none have reached the level of success that Jennifer has. Jennifer is the first Hispanic female to build an enviable career of starring in mainstream movies—in fact, she is the highest paid Hispanic actress in history. She has sold over 35 million records world-wide. She is one of few Hispanic women to be seen constantly on mainstream magazines and to star on mainstream television.

Jennifer is also the first Hispanic singer to venture into R&B/ Hip-Hop while infusing it with Spanish vibes to also stay connected with her strong Latin audience. Jennifer bridged a gap in music that sparked many other singers to pair up with performers of different genres. The entertainment world was forced to realize that an entire group had been shut out in the past before Jennifer stepped on the scene.

Track 1: "Let's Get Loud"

On July 24, 1970 in the Bronx neighborhood known as "Castle Hill", a Puerto-Rican couple, David, a computer operations specialist, and Quadalupe Lopez, a kindergarten teacher, welcomed their second daughter, Jennifer, into the world. She joined her older sister Lynda and was later joined by another sister, Leslie.

Quadalupe and David had a strong commitment to family life, and raised their girls in a strict household. The rules they set were to be followed throughout their entire upbringing. The family was also very involved in their Puerto-Rican traditions and heritage. The Lopez parents realized that their daughters needed to be educated not only about the beauty of their culture, but also about the problems they would face because of it.

Living in the United States, and wanting the best for their daughters in the present and future, caused David and Quadalupe to decide that the girls should speak English both at home and in public. They did not want to fall into any of the negative stereotypes of a Hispanic family, and therefore strove to be a "conventional" American family. The two were also explicit in teaching their daughters how important it was for them to get a decent education as well as the value of hard work.

Although the Lopez household was a strict one, the entire family knew how to have fun. Their daily lives revolved around music as it livened the household during homework, chores, and even prayer.

Of the three Lopez sisters, Jennifer especially grasped the love of music. While her mother loved Diana Ross and the Supremes, Jennifer opted for the cool sounds of The Sugarhill Gang. Singing and Dancing were two things that really made Jennifer happy.

All three of the girls had amazing musical talent, but being the middle child caused Jennifer to ache for attention, and she became much more unpredictable and aggressive with her talent. She was animated in showing off her abilities and she loved to be watched. It was this personality trait that made Jennifer's parents decide to let her take singing and dancing lessons at five years old.

Jennifer was unique in the fact that she was never afraid to fail. This allowed her to try many new things that she otherwise would have been afraid to do. She danced, sang, and played sports, all while excelling in school and seriously practicing her Catholic faith.

As Jennifer grew into a teenager, she realized that many of her interests were not set in the guidelines of her strict household; in fact, many of the things she became interested in were the exact opposite of what her parents wanted for her. Although she was fifteen and still sharing the same bed with both of her sisters, she was maturing into a woman, and becoming increasingly inter-ested in boys. She soon found that her parents' rules did not coincide with what she wanted to do, and began to defy them.

She replaced her need to be noticed by her parents with a need to be loved by a young man—a boy named David Cruz became a very important part of her teenage life. Jennifer did everything she could to be with David, including sneaking out of the house just to meet him.

Track 2: "Dance With Me"

Jennifer began exhibiting her musical talents in her teens by performing in a slew of musical productions such as *Oklahoma, Jesus Christ Superstar,* and *Golden Musicals of Broadway.* She had her first small screen break at age sixteen when she landed the role of "Myra" in *My Little Girl* (1986).

Although all of these experiences opened her eyes to the world of entertainment, it was not until 1990 that Jennifer got her biggest break: a spot as a Fly Girl dancer on Fox's hit sketch comedy show *In Living Color.*

This show was unique in the sense that it attempted to differentiate itself from other sketch comedy shows by heavily catering to a young, hip-hop crowd. The producers decided to have a popular hip-hop artist perform at the end of each show, but decided that what would make the show *especially* innovative, would be to have a troop of hip-hop dancers perform throughout the show.

Jennifer was happy to have been offered the part of one of the Fly Girls, but was scared about leaving everything that she had grown used to, living in New York. The shows producer and fellow New Yorker, Keenan Ivory Wayans, convinced her that moving to LA would be the best thing for her career. David Cruz further encouraged the twenty-year-old Jennifer by moving to LA with her.

Jennifer enjoyed dancing as a Fly Girl the entire time that *In Living Color* was on the air; however, being exposed to the studios in Hollywood made her desire a role that was more in the forefront.

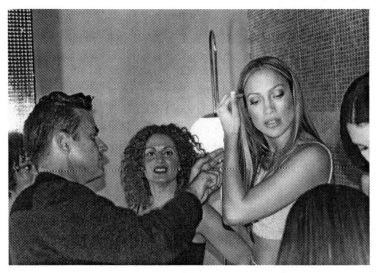

Track 3: "I've Been Thinking"

In 1993, Jennifer partook in two television roles. She played the role of 'Rosie Romero' in the television movie, "Nurses on the Line: The Crash of Flight 7", and also 'Melinda Lopez' in a television series called "Second Chances". Neither role was ground-breaking or lasting.

She decided to again embrace her love for dancing, and landed a spot as a dancer in Janet Jackson's "That's The Way Love Goes" video. Although she enjoyed being a part of the extremely popular video, she still desired to be involved in a project in which she was able to play a more impressive and forefront role.

She then thought that her acting career was bound to take off when she got a bit part on the African-American show "South Central" starring Tina Lifford and Larenz Tate. The series was supposed to be a stepping stone for the Fox network, depicting the violent side of growing up black in the hood. Unfortunately, the show's ratings were poor, and it was canceled after its first season. In 1994, she again played the role of 'Melinda Lopez' in another television series called "Hotel Malibu". This was yet another disappointment for Jennifer as it was not successful.

Jennifer had appeared in many television events by the end of 1994, but she was hardly noticeable in the small roles she had taken. Jennifer was receiving no publicity and the parts she took were on the borderline of negative Hispanic stereotypes. She had grown tired of Hispanics being typecast as immigrants, drunks, maids, and drug dealers throughout the years; she no longer wanted to perpetuate the stereotype. Little did she know, that would all change very soon.

Jennifer was finally going to get her chance to succeed and show the entire world what she was made of. In 1995 Jennifer landed the role of 'Maria Sanchez' in *Mi Familia (My Family)*, starring Jimmy Smits, Edward James Olmos, and Esai Morales. The film's director, Gregory Nava, was so impressed with Jennifer's work in *Mi Familia*, that he kept her name handy for future projects. Jennifer continued to play in Hispanic films, but she knew crossing over to a mainstream audience was needed if she wanted to become a big success. Jennifer had always been raised to be proud of who and what she was. She felt she could do this *and* crossover at the same time.

In 1995, at age 25, her relationship with David Cruz had ended and Jennifer was a full-grown woman. She wanted to stand out and she hadn't accomplished that in her latest roles. Jennifer tried her best to seek out roles in mainstream films.

Her perseverance led to triumph and her wishes were answered. Jennifer had searched, but no matter how many times she had been rejected, she persisted until she received a role in a mainstream film.

Track 4: "I'm Gonna Be Alright"

Jennifer got her first chance to really shine in the movie *Money Train* alongside two of the top actors of the nineties, Wesley Snipes and Woody Harrelson.

The film that cost $60 million to make opened on November of 1995, but grossed only $35.1 million dollars. Critics blamed the dismal figures on a dense movie with a half-empty plot. Others blamed it on the terrible publicity that the film received after it seemed that someone mimicked the film by setting a New York City subway token booth on fire. Soon after, Senator Bob Dole issued a boycott on the film due to a clerk being attacked and seriously injured in what he believed to be another instance of mimicking the film.

Jennifer kept her head held high, and went on to star in the movie *Jack* with Robin Williams. A year later, she played a Cuban mistress in "Blood and Wine" starring Jack Nicholson. Like *Money Train* before them, both of these films were disappointments at the box office, and most of all to Jennifer.

Although she was being featured in major Hollywood films, her roles were always overshadowed by the A-list celebrities that she worked with. Furthermore, the films never hit the anticipated mark of success. She finally decided to stray from her past formula of signing onto "guaranteed blockbusters" starring popular actors, and take on a new challenge. She made a choice to take on a role that would not only further her career, but would also bridge the gap between the Hispanic community and Hollywood.

Jennifer again had the opportunity to work with director Greg Nava when she accepted the lead role in the bio-pic *Selena*. The film created a lot of buzz and finally gave Jennifer the recognition she desired. Ironically, Jennifer played the role of real life musician Selena Quintanilla-Perez, who like she one day

would, attempted to acquire not only a culture fan base, but also a pop culture fan base. Logically, all participants in the *Selena* movie thought that if Selena could have crossover appeal, why not her Jennifer?

Jennifer felt extra stress to ensure the films success because it was such an emotional project. Various members of Selena's family were involved in the project and even watched during the shooting of the film. Despite her chance at stardom and her admiration for Selena, her respect for making a project that Selena's family would really be proud of made it extremely important for Jennifer to do her best.

The family had nothing to worry about. Jennifer received rave reviews for her performance in *Selena*, and only made the performance more convincing with something she had no control over: her uncanny resemblance to the Tejana singer. The film was highly regarded by critics all over the country, and Selena's memory proved the ideal project for a top-rated film.

At once, everything in Jennifer's life began to change. She was being shoved into numerous interviews, and upcoming movie proposals. Through all of the events that kept Jennifer busy, she was somehow able to establish a relationship with a new man, model Ojani Noa. The relationship became very serious very quickly.

Jennifer's personal life accelerated at a speed rapid enough to keep up with her professional life. Ojani let Jennifer know just how serious he was about her by proposing marriage at the *Selena* wrap party in 1996. A year later they were happily married and within a year of their nuptials, they were happily divorced.

She strengthened her box office resume by landing roles in *Anaconda,* Oliver Stone's *U Turn,* and *Out of Sight* with George Clooney. She became the highest paid Latina actress earning between two and five million dollars per film. She even joined the modern phenomenon of lending one's voice to a feature-length animated film when she read for *Antz* in 1998.

Track 5: "Could This Be Love"

A trend that is very interesting in Jennifer Lopez's life is that through each major transition, there is the entrance of a romantic partner. When she got her first break on *In Living Color*, David was by her side as her support system. When she first reached the acclaim in Hollywood that she had always desired, she married Ojani. The next transition in her life would not occur unlike any of the others.

Although Jennifer was seriously pursuing her acting career in LA, her love for music and New York never left her heart. Her next deep relationship would be with a man whose love for

these two things probably outranked Jennifer's. This man exuded the New York lifestyle and was at the top of the music game in the 90's. This man was Sean "P Diddy" Combs.

The two met when Jennifer appeared in Diddy's video "Been Around the World". She was the subject of his interest in the video, and soon became the subject of his interest in real life as well. To some, they were the most mismatched couple in music, but they were constantly seen together, and seemed to have a wonderful connection.

Dating Sean inspired Jen to pursue a project that wouldn't involve a script or movie screen. In 1998, Jennifer decided to take up her favorite talent, singing. She had abandoned this childhood love for film roles, and since starring in such a music oriented film as *Selena,* the craving to sing was stronger than ever. Luckily, "Jennifer Lopez" was already a household name, and instead of having to go through the hassles that most aspiring musicians do, she had record companies scrambling to sign her to their label.

Although her struggle to receive a contract was not very difficult, she realized that it would not be quite as easy to convince the public that she was capable of success in the music industry. She knew that many would think that she only received a contract because she was pretty or because she had already established her name in entertainment business. Yet, she wanted to prove that the power of her contract was actually due to her musical talent.

Jennifer chose to sign with Sony Music Entertainment and the process of writing and recording *On The 6* began. The first album consisted of fourteen R&B and Latin singles that would make Jennifer's debut her biggest album released. She co-wrote four of the songs and was helped by some of the industry's finest producers: Gloria Estefan, Darkchild, and her boyfriend P Diddy. The mixture of R&B and Latin music created an untouched trend that proved highly successful.

The first single, "If You Had My Love" was immediately in circulation at radio stations. Her album, *On the 6*, named after the train she used to ride in the Bronx, was doing very well by the end of 1998.

The album continued to flourish in 1999 as she released "No Me Ames", a duet with Marc Anthony that stayed atop the Latin Billboard charts for seven weeks. At the same time, "If You Had My Love" went to number one. The video was nominated for four MTV Music Awards including "Best Female Video" and "Best New Artist", and soon after, the album went triple platinum. So far, Jennifer was proving the skeptics wrong and burning up the airwaves from MTV to BET for weeks without budging.

She topped music channel charts, radio airplay charts and even magazine polls for Best New Artist. She released "Waiting for Tonight" and experienced that same chart topping success that her previous releases had earned. The month of December had approached again, and Jennifer's music had been consistently ruling the airwaves for a year.

It was also in this month that Jennifer and Sean's relationship began to unravel. While Jennifer's musical career was at an all time high, her personal life and public persona were not. Many people close to Jennifer did not think highly of her relationship with P Diddy. Although a very serious and successful business man, he had gained a "bad boy" reputation for his role in the East Coast/ West Coast rivalry—a rivalry, which many believe, led to the deaths of rap icons Tupac and the Notorious B.I.G. The naysayers' fears were not quelled when in December of 1999, Jennifer and Sean were arrested after a shooting occurred at a New York City nightclub.

Jennifer was held for fourteen hours before being released. Sean was charged with possession of a stolen gun and had to appear before a trial. Shyne, a new rapper on the Bad Boy label, was sentenced to life in prison for killing a man that night.

Both reputations were being slandered and Jennifer feared for her career. The two kept the emotional nature of their relationship at an arms length from the press while Sean dealt with his

legal obligations. Jennifer continued to appear at awards shows and did guest appearances on television. During this time, Jennifer and Sean's relationship slowly began to deteriorate.

As we have learned from following Jennifer's life, this could only mean that she was finishing a phase in her life and was about to enter another.

Track 6: "Ain't It Funny"

After the nightclub fiasco, Jen's career hit a rough patch of road. The media and the public seemed tirelessly more interested in her legal issues than her career endeavors. She was constantly defending herself from slanderous accusations while trying to reestablish her positive persona.

Though much of the media attention was negative, it did nothing but spark the public's interest in all things Lopez. She was awarded the lead role in *The Cell* as *On the 6*'s record sales continued to soar.

In February, she released "Feelin' So Good" featuring P Diddy which also went to top 10, as the previously released music continued to gain acclaim. She received a "Best Dance Recording" Grammy nomination for "Waiting for Tonight" and won two Billboard Latin Awards.

The media hadn't stopped her flow. Jennifer stopped talking and kept singing. In April, Jennifer was named *FHM Magazine's* "Sexiest Woman in the World". No longer did you have to be blond, blue-eyed, and skinny to be seen as beautiful. Jenny was a thick, curvy, large-hipped bombshell who was known as "La Guitarra" (the guitar) for her hourglass shape. Most importantly, Jennifer herself was proud of her body.

She had so much style that she was awarded the "Versace Award" at the VH-1 Vogue Fashion Awards. It was at this point that, Jennifer changed the face of beauty by bringing the beautiful body types of Latin and Black women to the attention of mainstream America.

Track 7: "My Love Won't Cost A Thing"

Jennifer knew how important it was to stay fresh and innovative in the music industry, and decided that she should keep her fans guessing and interested by tweaking her image. She dyed her hair and renamed herself J.Lo. It was a nickname that fans on the street had been calling Jennifer since she started singing in 1999. Jennifer was flattered and opted to use the name for her sophomore album, and ultimately, herself. It was quite catchy, and soon everyone from Robin Leach to Barbara Walters was using the acronym.

J.Lo's relationship with Sean had become especially rocky right around the time that she released the first single, "My Love Won't Cost a Thing" from her sophomore album in December

2000. The content of the song caused speculation that it was a message to her millionaire boyfriend, Diddy. The combination of this speculated drama, the sassy message for independent women, and the danceable beat helped propel this hit song to the top 10. Amazingly, she was still riding the waves of success of *On the 6,* and found herself promoting two albums at once.

It was around this time Jenny had grown accustomed to the finer things in life. The most popular designers constantly sent her designs to wear to events. Even during her own time, she was always cloaked in the finest clothes, furs and jewels. Her new image doted on cash and she sparkled from head to toe in diamond rings and ankle bracelets. J.Lo had taught Jennifer how to live the good life.

With the release of J.Lo, it seemed that Jennifer had more confidence and understood what she wanted within her career. Once again, Jennifer mixed music with movies as she appeared in *The Wedding Planner* with Matthew McConaughey. Jennifer had become such an important star, that the role she played in "The Wedding Planner" was scripted especially for her.

Unfortunately, her personal life was not as sweet as her professional life, and in February 2001, she and Sean officially broke up. Although no one but the couple knew exactly why the two ended their relationship, it was no secret that the legal battles put a great stress on their union.

Although she was dealing with the heartache of her break up, her professional life continued to soar. She released the Christina Milian written "Play", which also climbed to top 10. She signed a deal with NBC for a sitcom and to perform various concert specials. Somehow, with all that Jennifer was facing in music and television, she was able to find time to star with James Caviezel in *Angel Eyes.*

ℑrack 8: "ℑ'm ℜeal"

Being in a deep relationship with powerful business man Sean Combs enlightened Jennifer. Like her business mogul ex, Jennifer decided to start her own clothing and accessory company, also called J.Lo, in April 2001. She specialized in fashionable clothing for women of *all* sizes. Being a curvy woman herself, Jennifer not only knew how difficult it was to find trendy clothing that fit well, but also that women of all sizes were just as interested in style as their twiggy sisters. In an interview with E! Online, she said she felt that in the fashion world, "the voluptuous woman [was] almost ignored", and that in her clothing, "everyone [would get] to be sexy". Having a keen interest in fashion since childhood, clothing design was yet another talent that Jennifer decided to share with the world. Jennifer again succeeded in widening the parameters of the definitions of what was alluring and beautiful.

Jennifer's official entrance into the fashion world sparked interest in several companies, and by the end of 2001, she not only had her own clothing line, but also a fragrance, "Glow", and a contract with L'Oreal.

However, one of the most important lessons that Diddy taught Jennifer (and the world) was the power of "The Remix". She released "I'm Real" which immediately found a spot in the top 40, and then decided to outdo it by remixing the song with Ja Rule as a guest rapper. The song was an instant hit which climbed to the top 10.

However, the song received a backlash from outraged fans and non-fans alike for her use of the word "nigga" in the song. Many people thought that she had gotten too comfortable within the black community and were offended by the racist remark. Jennifer defended herself endlessly and was terribly hurt by the lash she encountered. She insisted that Ja Rule wrote the remix and that if she had to do it again, she would have used better judgment.

Once again, the publicity, negative or not, boosted her popularity as *J.Lo* went triple platinum. She saw the quick success of this track as a sign for a business opportunity, and chose to release an entire remix album, *J to tha L-O! The Remixes,* which went platinum.

Track 9: "Jenny From The Block"

Jennifer began to release videos for the *J.Lo* album. One of her most significant videos would be the one on which she met her future husband Chris Judd. Chris was one of her back-up dancers, and they shared an immediate connection. In fact, in September 2001, after only eight months of knowing each other, they were married.

Although thoroughly involved with her current relationship, she continued to invest in the business lessons that she had learned from P Diddy. With the success of his restaurant "Justin's", she decided that one could not go wrong with the combination of delicious food and superstar owner. In April 2002, Jennifer opened "Madre's" in Southern California—a restaurant specializing in innovative Puerto-Rican and Cuban cuisine. On the contrary, her marriage to Chris was not as successful. The romance fizzled as quickly as it began, and in July 2002, she filed for divorce.

Her bad luck with relationships did not stop her career success. In addition to maintaining her music career, restaurant, and clothing company, she juggled two movies. She spent the following months continuing to work on both the feminine-charged *Enough* and *Gigli* with Ben Affleck, which began production in the end of 2001.

The romance in the script of *Gigli* led to a real life romance, and not long after her split from Chris, news broke to the world that she and Ben were an official couple. According to newspapers and magazines, a lot of people had tired of Jennifer's short-lived relationships; thus, instead of being happy for her new romance, the public began to wait around to see if it would actually last.

After releasing three hit albums back-to-back-to-back within a three year time span, Jennifer found it only fitting to release a fourth album. However, this time around, the public was not as enthused. She was accused of forgetting where she had come from. She was labeled as superficial and a sellout who was obsessed with her money and looks. It was a rude awakening. Though Jennifer still appealed to millions of fans, her career could not withstand such a switch. She gave up the blond hair, toned down the make-up, and her loveable Latin features resurfaced.

She further assured her audiences that she was still the same down-to-earth babe from the Bronx by releasing "Jenny from the Block" as the first song from *This is Me...Then*. The message was enhanced by the accompaniment of one of New York's grittiest and most talented acts, The Lox. Each lyric in the song seemed to be an explanation defending her actions, fame, and how she'd come to live her life in the last three years.

The song was an instantaneous hit, and *This Was Me...Then* went double platinum in less than three months. She appeared in the film *Maid in Manhattan*, a modern day Cinderella story, and was ecstatic as it earned nineteen million at the box office its opening weekend. It was the success of this film that made Jennifer realize that she had really made it into mainstream Hollywood. Romantic comedies are generally films that have mass appeal and star some of Hollywood's most popular, white, leading ladies. In fact, Julia Roberts was first approached for the role before Jennifer accepted it. She had entered the upper echelon of big screen leading ladies.

Her music career also continued to flourish as she was the recipient of an American Music Award nomination. However, though her professional and personal life seemed to be in a whirlwind of triumph, she was unaware of the consequence of the influx of overexposure that would occur in the near future due to the media's ongoing coverage of her popularity.

Track 10: "Dear Ben"

Regardless of all of the fame and success Jennifer has had within her career, all she ever wanted was love. Having two marriages end so quickly and her relationship with Sean Combs trashed by the media served as life lessons for Jennifer to be more private with her relationships, and to be patient enough to wait for the right man. Unfortunately, being deeply in love can cause even the strongest person to ignore the important lessons they have learned.

The public was suddenly bombarded with Jennifer's newest relationship with Ben Affleck; they attended numerous events arm-in-arm and were plastered on the cover of every celebrity magazine for months. The couple was inseparable and it did not take long until the unit was referred to as "Bennifer".

For the first time, Jennifer drastically broke down the boundary from her personal life and her professional life. She and Ben played love interests in both *Gigli* and *Jersey Girl*. She released her video for "Jenny from the Block", and made viewers double take when they saw a scene with Ben lounging in his bathrobe. She even dedicated a song on her album to him, and appropriately named it "Dear Ben".

Perhaps it was this overexposure of the couple that led to *Gigli* being one of the summer of 2003's biggest flops. The public had scene enough of "Bennifer" without their consent; nobody wanted to pay for it.

The failure of *Gigli* did not slow Jennifer. She booked various performances, including the Soul Train Awards. She made cameo appearances on one of her favorite sitcoms, *Will and Grace.* She even worked on a song with U2's Bono between video shoots.

With Ben Affleck she seemed to be a different woman. Although she claimed to still be "Jenny from the Block", she had traded in her jeans and velour sweatsuits for elegant gowns made by Prada and Versace. She signed a contract with Louis Vuitton and became the company's main print model. She was proving that she had matured; she was sophisticated and completely aware—ready for every step that she made in the future. Ben proposed to her with a beautiful, $1.2 million pink diamond, and the world counted down the days to the wedding.

For the first time, Jennifer gave her relationship time to develop, and began to see (with the help of the media) that she and Ben were not as compatible as she thought. Their styles, practices, and even sports teams were polar opposites. Ben preferred to be comfortable in casual clothing, while Jennifer liked to dress to impress. Ben had enjoyed drinking and gambling, while Jennifer was strictly against each. Lastly, Jennifer represented the New York Yankee's while Ben was a life long fan of the team's biggest rival, the Boston Red Sox. As petty as some of them may seem, the differences mattered, and they began to pour out as the relationship progressed.

The wedding was postponed, and ultimately canceled. Jennifer, who had always been able to use any type of press to her advantage, was unable to control the effect it had on her relationship. Having been so sure that Ben was the answer to the picture perfect life she so desperately sought, Jennifer was completely devastated.

ℑrack 11: "Secretly"

J.Lo decided again to make a change and dropped the moniker that she had become known as. The name, "J.Lo" had taken on a persona, and she felt she needed to reestablish herself as the person she wanted to be, and no longer play into the role that the public had set for her.

Jennifer focused on the things that made her feel the happiest and the most complete. She poured her energy into her restaurant ensuring that it remained number one on the finest dining lists. She added to her entrepreneur status by creating a lingerie line under her J.Lo label. She delved back into her familial relationships by deciding to produce a talk show on Universal Domestic Television involving her sister, Lynda. She became an active political speaker stressing the importance of using one's vote. Yet, most importantly, she continued to give to and support charities such as the "Little Angel Bunny Foundation" and "Artists Against Aids Worldwide", that help fight against child abuse and AIDS, respectively.

As Jennifer began to rediscover the activities she enjoyed the most and began to surround herself with the people she loved the most, she found herself again in the company of Marc Anthony. As a bonus for working on her latest film, *Shall We Dance?*, she was to record a song with Marc Anthony for the film's soundtrack.

She first met Marc after her rise to fame in *Selena*, when he was interested in casting the new star in one of his videos. Savvy Jennifer only agreed to do so if the Latin superstar would lend his talent as a guest star on her debut album. Thus, the chart topper "No Me Ames" was born and a wonderful friendship was established.

Jennifer, newly single, and Marc going through a divorce, saw that they had an opportunity to work on a romance that was never possible before. However, Jennifer had learned her lesson about the frailty of combining celebrity and personal relationships, and made a vow to stay tight-lipped about the situation. When David Letterman questioned her about the relationship on his show, she completely avoided the issue by changing the subject. In fact, she is so private about her relationship with Anthony that she has neither verified nor denied that she and Anthony were wed in June 2004… less than a year after the anticipated wedding date with Ben.

Despite the uncertainty of the nuptials between Marc and Jen, the two have attended many affairs together, thrown parties for each other, and even bought homes together. Marc is also constantly seen on the set of Jennifer's next due film, *Monster-in-Law*, set to be in theaters in May of 2005. There is further speculation that Jennifer is pregnant; but, despite the validity of this claim, she has said that she is definitely ready to start a family. She has made a vow to stay quiet about her personal life and recently said in an interview with *Rolling Stone* magazine, "Your soul is so public and open and out there for everybody. There is no privacy. At the end of the day, you really have to fight to keep certain things sacred so that they survive." Still, the public awaits proof that Jennifer is capable of having success in her relationships as well as in her profession.

Due to her desire to focus on having children, Jennifer has slowed down over the past year, but she has not stopped. She and Anthony are expected to co-produce a movie about salsa singer Hector Lavoe under Jennifer's production company, Nuyorican Productions, in the near future. She is also expected to release her fifth album, *Rebirth,* in March, 2005 with "Get Right" as the album's first track.

Although Jennifer's appeal as an entertainer varies from person to person, all people have no choice but to respect and admire her smart business sense. She has crossed countless boundaries, and seized business opportunities that people before her had no idea about or were afraid to invest in. She has helped to tear down the invisible box of beauty that has existed in the United States for centuries, and shown that women's appealing qualities are so broad that they could never fit in a box anyway. And most importantly, she has made these important marks in history and pop culture all while doing what she has enjoyed most throughout her entire life: entertaining.

Through her perseverance and talent, Jennifer fought to be seen as more than a Hispanic female from the Bronx. She has led a path for many to follow and she has created a legacy that no one, Latino or other, can replace. No matter what the future holds, Jennifer Lopez will always be known as a female pioneer of achievement and the woman who made the world look twice.

Mya

Mya

Mya Harrison is an artist that has demanded respect from the very beginning of her career. The titles of her first two singles, "It's All about Me" and "Moving On", speak for themselves. With the introduction of the *Mya* album in 1998, we were also introduced to a strong young woman that motivated other women to join her in asserting their independence and demanding respect.

Although Mya tantalizes viewers with her beauty, sex appeal and dancing abilities, audiences appreciate her most and identify with the messages within her songs. Mya's music is often light-hearted and catchy; however, it boasts of independence, self-esteem, and a call for respect. Men revere her message while women relate to it.

Fans can also easily relate to Mya because behind her glamorous persona, she is still an everyday woman. She, like every other young woman, has dealt with self-esteem issues and has often felt like an underdog in many situations. She's had her heart broken and her confidence shattered. She's felt alone and has been afraid to take the risks involved in doing something that she always wanted to do. However, she harnessed her emotions, and learned from her experiences in order to become the successful woman that she is today.

Track 1: " It's All About Me"

On October 10, 1979 in Washington D.C., an Italian accountant named Theresa, and an African-American R&B

singer, Sherman, welcomed their first child. From the moment that Mya Marie Harrison was born, her parents could sense that she was very special, and found it only fitting to name her "Mya" in honor of famed novelist Maya Angelou. Mya was soon joined by brothers Nigel and Chaz, and the family moved from D.C. to Maryland.

It wasn't long before Mya began to show her amazing talents for dance. Mya's role of entertaining the world started when she was just two years old while dancing in the reflecting pool between the Washington Monument and Lincoln Memorial. Sherman and Theresa were blown away by their little daughter's feet and it wasn't long before the couple enrolled Mya in a ballet school.

Mya also showed interests in gymnastics and baton twirling and became involved in both of these activities as well. At age 10, Mya began to feel that her extensive training in so many challenging activities was causing her to miss out on her childhood. Mya decided that the best idea would be to relax, and enjoy the freedom of being a little girl again.

It didn't take long until Mya realized that dancing was not the only stress that she had in her life. She soon found that the teasing from her peers was far more stressful than any of her most challenging dance practices, routines, or performances. The stress that dance had in her life was far easier to overcome because it was physical; the stress that her teasing peers burdened her with bruised her ego.

Children made fun of Mya's biracial background, bushy hair, thick eyebrows, hairy arms, braces, and skinny body. She was called "Unibrow", "Hairy Harrison", "Metal Mouth", and "Zebra" by the bullies. When the mockers ran out of physical attributes to pick on, they focused on taunting Mya about being poor and shy. Mya found school to be torturous, and realized that fitting in was "easier said than done".

Mya felt that her only choice was to withdraw from the school crowd and distribute her attention elsewhere. She kept a journal at home to sort out her problems and insecurities. School became her top priority, as she began to focus strongly on her education and soon found herself an honor student. Although not long before she had thought that being a " normal" child was what she longed for the most, she realized that what was "natural" and "normal" to *her* was the art of dance—her need to dance was a feeling that could not be diminished. Mya quickly delved back into dancing and soon found it was exactly what she needed to get rid of the pain.

Track 2: "We're Gonna Make You Dance"

Dancing helped Mya become stronger and rebuild her self-esteem. Although she may have felt that the teasing children were superior to her on the school playground, she knew that in dancing, she was unbeatable. Mya was sparked by an

inner urge and encouraged by her parents to seek out her dance talents to see how far the art could take her.

Like most adolescents, Mya approached her teen years with uncertainty. Smartly, she harnessed her uncertainty and began to pursue new interests. She became fascinated with tap dancing and began to take classes. She also began to experiment in clothing and fashion design.

Mya became so deeply involved with her artistic outlets that school didn't seem as threatening as it had in previous years. She honed her Hip-Hop skills and began intently focusing on tap until it became her biggest priority. Tap dancing became Mya's way of communicating with herself. When Mya danced, she felt like she was the only person in the world. On the dance floor, her shyness evaporated, and people began to take notice.

She then tried out for Savion Glover's Washington Tap Residency. Being one of the most prolific and popular tappers of today, she knew that this school would be a great step in excelling in tap. Unfortunately, although she had the skill, she lacked the knowledge of technical tap, and was turned down two years in a row. Mya did not let this discourage her, and on the third year, she was accepted into TWA (Tappers with

Attitude), a group consisting of teens from all backgrounds, at age eleven. Being a member of this group opened the doors for Mya to do what she most wanted to do: perform.

Mya was soon invited to tap in various live performances. She performed at the Kennedy Center, the Lincoln Center, the Smithsonian, and the Shakespeare Center. Mya was also invited to perform in the show, "Scorch Marks on The Floor" where her talents became highly recognized. In 1992, at age thirteen, Mya was an Honorable Mention recipient of the Steve Condos Scholarship—a scholarship which honored the best new talent by picking one recipient annually.

Although Mya had not made it into Savion Glover's residency, he was so impressed with Mya's dancing style that he invited her to his Boston Tap Residency for a three-night performance at The Strand Theater in 1993. That summer, Mya studied tap and jazz in New York City at the Broadway Dance Center and Woodpeckers.

Mya heightened her knowledge of tap by beginning to choreograph and teach classes in her Maryland area. All of her hard work again paid off in 1994 when she received a Tap America Scholarship, and had the opportunity to share the stage with numerous tap talents, including tap legend Gregory Hines.

Track 3: "Best of Me"

Although Mya was flourishing in the tap world, she had another issue to deal with once high school started: she thought of herself as undeveloped and skinny while the other girls had started to develop womanly figures for their age. She found this extremely frustrating as her interest in boys began to grow. To make matters more difficult, Mya's parents limited she and her brothers' social activities so that they could concentrate on their musical activities. Any chance that she had to establish a relationship with a guy was quickly foiled, as her father closely screened and monitored all calls received from boys.

Mya found that once again she was not able to enjoy the "normal" experience of most people her age; she regretted not being able to date. Valentine's Day was especially hard for her, and she began to hate walking down the romantically decorated halls knowing that she had no sweetheart with whom to share the day. Year after year, she wished she could avoid the spectacle.

As always, Mya found peace in her solace: art. She allowed her natural artistic abilities to fill her dissatisfaction. She began to draw and sold her work for five dollars apiece at school. The students raved about her beautiful drawings, and soon she had acquired a sizable income. For once she felt accepted and appreciated amongst her peers. She also continued to focus on dancing and playing the violin and piano.

Though Mya had achieved and grown immensely from her various forms of art, she still felt empty. Her childhood memories of singing to her favorite albums haunted her. Mya's household had always been a haven of entertainment and talent—a musical celebration. Her father's career had had a lasting affect on her life. Although she loved playing instruments, drawing, and especially dancing, she realized that singing was the artistic element that her soul longed for.

Mya participated in Black Entertainment Television's Teen Summit and began working on her hip-hop skills. It was not long before Mya realized her voice was as gifted as her feet. She practiced singing to Mary J. Blige tapes and began showcasing her talent. Although she knew she had a beautiful voice, singing professionally had not crossed her mind.

Mya decided that once she graduated from Eleanor Roosevelt High School, she would enroll at the University of Maryland and major in Speech Communications. It wasn't until Mya met Dru Hill in 1996 at a Grammy party that she began thinking about turning her talent into a career.

Of all of Mya's artistic capabilities, singing was the hardest for her to tackle. Even though she had been performing in front of crowds her whole life, she was still very shy. In fact, she was so shy about her desire to sing that she hadn't even *expressed* it to anyone. She understood that a major step in maturing into a woman would be overcoming her timidity; she had to make her parents aware of her desire if she wanted to satisfy this craving in her soul.

Her love for tap would have to take a backseat for her to truly give a chance to singing. The risk was especially scary because Mya had no experience of singing confidently in public. Singing played intimidating mental games with her that dancing did not.

As a child, she wanted to sing at her grandmother's church. Each time Mya attended the service, she was hypnotized by the dominant and vibrant sounds of the choir. Unfortunately, she lacked the confidence to sing in front of the congregation. She always had the urge, but not the esteem, to sing in school programs. In fact, she was so intimidated by her voice that even her own father hadn't heard her sing a note until she was fourteen years old. When Mya finally expressed her interest to her parents, they agreed that she would benefit from the personal enrichment of becoming a professional singer. With her parents' support, Mya decided to actively pursue her wishes.

She began to train her voice, and before long, her father had her recording demo tapes singing Mary J. Blige and Jackson 5 songs. Her father's connections within his own musical career greatly helped when he brought Mya's singing ability to the attention of Haqq Islam, Interscope Records/Universal Music CEO and President. Haqq was so impressed he presented Mya with her first record deal.

Most teenagers would have stopped their lives in its track after signing a recording contract, but Mya did not. She still wanted to go to college and shortly after signing the contract with Interscope/ Universal, she followed her plan by enrolling in the University of Maryland. Mya soon found that, signing a record deal was not something that one could take lightly.

Track 4: "Now or Never"

She was now owned by Interscope and many of her plans had to be put on hold if she wanted to succeed as a singer. Mya saw that she could not fulfill such obligations and college at the same time.

She hadn't even recorded her first song and already she had to make her first sacrifice. Mya passed up an education at the University of Maryland and headed into the entertainment world.

The last thing the R&B industry needed was another wannabe. It seemed like getting a deal was turning out to be the easiest part for Mya; finding a place in the unforgiving world of show business would be even harder. Mya remembered all the times she felt she would never succeed at anything. She remembered all the times she had been disrespected and disliked because of who she was. She used these past experiences to fuel her drive for success and made a vow not to turn back, no matter how frightening it was.

However, though she was prepared to face any hardships that the music industry might throw her way, she was not prepared for the dilemma her family was soon to face. Mya's mother was diagnosed with cancer. She decided to be optimistic about the situation and searched for whatever positive lessons she could learn from it. She said, "I once read that 10% of life includes our experiences, 90% is how we deal with them," and decided to use this situation to prove the philosophy.

Her mother's battle with cancer caused her to realize that life is too short to be caught up in other people's perceptions. Regardless of all of the lessons that she would learn throughout her career, it was this lesson that was the most beneficial to her personal well-being. She grew from this experience and became even stronger. Luckily, her mother also became stronger as she defeated the cancer with the help of chemotherapy.

Track 5: "After The Rain"

Her focus was rewarded when her self-titled album was released in April 1998. The first single, "It's All About Me," featuring Sisqo, hit the top 40. She landed a spot on the *Bullworth* soundtrack and climbed into the top ten, performing "Ghetto Supastar (That's What You Are)" with Ol' Dirty Bastard and Pras. "Ghetto Supastar" was such a hit that it was nominated for two MTV Video Awards in 1998: Best Rap Video and Best Video from a Film.

Mya had continued success on her first album with the help of writing from Babyface on "My First Night with You", and a guest spot from Silkk the Shocker on "Movin On", which hit top 40 within a week of release. Although *Mya* went platinum, she still was not satisfied.

Mya wanted to learn the business side of the music industry. She read books about handling her business opportunities as well as the music; she knew that one had to know about the business in order to succeed in it. Mya's life seemed to be heading closer to her dreams, and she proved ready for the change. In 1998 there was not a place in black music where you did not see Mya's face or hear her songs.

Mya made hundreds of notable appearances and showed off her dancing skills. She received a Soul Train Music Award Nomination for "It's All About Me", and was the only female performer at the "Smokin' Grooves Tour" that year. Mya was seen on magazine covers and written about in articles for Teen, Seventeen, People, and Vibe Magazine. She was living high off of the fact that she had been named #88 Singles Artist of The Year, and had a hit album. As if that wasn't enough, Mya appeared in the film "In Too Deep," which starred Omar Epps and rapper LL Cool J.

Despite all of the recognition that she received from the media, it was the recognition from her peers and mentors that she truly valued. Mya became sought after by some of the music industry's biggest producers and song writers, including Babyface and Missy Elliot.

𝔗rack 6: "𝔊hetto 𝔖upastar"

With strong R&B vocals and super hip-hop tracks, Mya was labeled the new "Ghetto Princess"—she was the new "it" girl. However, even thought she was topping charts, she was not shielded from harsh criticism. Some said that Mya's fame was propelled by a lack of competition. Many of the veterans like Aaliyah, Brandy, and Monica, were taking breaks from music while seeking out other areas of entertainment. Mya had to prove that her success was not circumstantial, and that she could hold her own battling against these established performers. She focused on her dancing and live performances, and even the harshest Mya critics had to give her props for her talent and entertainment abilities.

And as the successful teen divas before her, Mya used her success in the music industry as a catapult to other areas of interest. Her love for fashion was exemplified when she became a spokeswoman for Bongo Jeans and received a Tommy Hilfiger lipstick shade in her name. Outside of the spotlight, Mya became a devoted speaker for teen and female issues.

Mya was a great mentor for young women because she had experienced many of the same things they had: she had battled with self-esteem and insecurity issues. She became involved with the advisory board of the Secret to Self Esteem Program, a program dedicated to the growth of strong young ladies and women. Mya's strategy of being taken seriously as a positive black woman was working on the charts and off. She had earned the respect of her peers, and by the end of 1998, Mya had sold two million records.

With the success she had on the *Bullworth* soundtrack with "Ghetto Supastar", Mya decided to enlist in another soundtrack project. The song was "Take Me There" on the *Rugrats* soundtrack and featured one of the hottest rappers at the time, Mase. Regardless of the fact that this song was for a children's movie, it was not long before it was a hit. "Take Me There" quickly hit the top ten, adding another successful hit to Mya's discography.

Track 7: "Take Me There"

In 1999, Mya went back to the studio to record "Fear of Flying". This album was more difficult than the first because she had to stay fresh by reinventing herself, and was up for a battle to outdo her toughest competition: herself. With the smoldering success of the first album, she knew she would have to step up her game to outshine it.

The most difficult part about recording her second album was determining what direction she wanted to take. The dilemma was only complicated by the fact that Mya's personal life had taken a strain. She was not surrounded by the support of her family as she was when she recorded her first album living with her family in Maryland. Instead, she was living alone in New York. Her parents were having problems of their own which resulted in a divorce at the end of 1999.

Mya's time was scarce. She was doing photo shoots, traveling, performing concerts and benefits, touring, appearing at charity gatherings, and giving speeches. Her solution to the stress was to take some time for herself, and embrace an activity that quieted her soul. She enrolled in swing and African dance classes and blew her instructors away learning the steps on the first time around.

Although she was beginning work on her second album, the success of her previous endeavors was still peaking. The appreciation for Mya's work really began to pour in when she was nominated in 1999 for a Grammy in the "Best Rap Performance by a Group or Duo" category for "Ghetto Supastar". Her next single, "My First Night with You" hit the top 40 as "Movin On" was nominated for the "Soul Train Lady of Soul Award" for R&B/Soul Song of the Year.

Through all of the excitement, Mya continued to relax her worn out mind and body. She danced, played guitar, read, and became a vegetarian. These actions strengthened her mind and body, and she began to grow the confidence of a woman. She became more comfortable with her figure and overall sex appeal. She admired the sophistication of styles worn by women from earlier generations and decided that was the style that she most identified with.

Mya's style of dress and music are dictated by the mood she's in. She has admitted that they way she looks in videos or magazines is not the way she looks naturally; when she's living her everyday life, she is wearing jeans and no make-up. She has also admitted that most of the time she can't even do her own hair or makeup. Although she is a celebrity, she is still a real person. If Mya is happy, the feeling is brought out in her dance moves and song writing. If her music is sad, it's because she is actually feeling sad. Mya's songs and dances are all products of her emotions. Her sophomore release would prove to be an eclectic compilation of her emotions.

Track 8: "Fear of Flying"

Mya opted for *Fear of Flying* as the title for her second release, because it gave insight on her emotions at the time. Although she had a platinum album and several top ten hits under her belt, she still had a lot to strive for, and ironically, still had a fear of success. In the *Real Detroit Weekly* she said, "Flying is a parallel to success and in order to be successful the way others define it, you usually have to give a bit of yourself up to fit that definition of what they call 'success'. Fear of flying is a fear of being successful. You have to be for yourself…Take that risk for yourself and be for yourself. "

Fear of Flying took Mya to new heights. Her sophomore release exemplified why fans truly appreciated her music. It was poetic, sexy, passionate, and most of all, it employed honest

sensitivity. From that moment on, Mya was more than the woman on the album cover—she was the producer of a project she held dear to her heart.

Mya revealed so much of her personal side in *Fear of Flying* that it brought fans closer to the artist herself; Mya had been granted the artistic freedom to write songs for the album as well as help with the choreography in the videos. Finally a woman, she was in control of her personal life, and she realized that is was time to call the shots in her career as well. She took charge and *Fear of Flying* ascended as Mya's most expressive release.

The first track, "Case of the Ex" was released in October 2000, debuting in the top 40. By November, the single hit the top 10. It reached number two on the Billboard Charts and stayed for three months. It glided through the "Hot 100" for thirty weeks and peaked at the top of the charts. "Case of the Ex" became the launching pad for *Fear of Flying*.

This album succeeded in a way that the first had not...it had crossover appeal. Mya was now a mainstream success and was awarded the spot of the # 46 Singles Artist of the Year. Being in the mainstream public eye accelerated her success as she was winning awards, participating in tributes, and working in films. She proved herself a well-rounded performer with flexible abilities.

Mya was suddenly a household name and was consistently a source of attraction on television and on tour. She performed on The Queen Latifah Show and on MTV's House of Style with Jadakiss. She performed at The World Music Awards, on BET's 106th & Park, and was showcased for the second year in a row as one of *Teen Magazine's* "25 Under 25". She toured internationally for her second album. After some time, the adrenaline wore thin, and the hectic lifestyle caught up with the singer. Mya was becoming tired, and suffered from high anxiety. She experienced sickness from being overseas, and extreme exhaustion.

Mya took time to heal and relax, and luckily, the album continued to sell itself. Besides the aural appeal of the music, fans really related to her messages. They were drawn in by her honesty and were able to connect with the way that she, as a woman, felt about herself.

Mya led by example; she showed that self-confidence and personal achievement can outweigh emotional obstacles. However, she was a human before a leader or an entertainer. She had her own emotional issues and psychological hang-ups.

Mya could stand up in front of a crowd of 11,000 people and sing in fishnet stockings and a lace bra, yet she was so shy that she preferred telephone and written interviews. However, when it came to her principles and morals, she was strong and unwavering. She, like all people, was a unique blend of strength and weakness.

Track 9: "Lady Marmalade"

In February 2001, Mya was hitting number 40 on the charts again... this time with "Free", a single from the *Bait* movie soundtrack. That same month, Mya was nominated for yet another award: the Soul Train Music Award for Best R&B/Soul Album for a female. *Fear of Flying* went platinum a month later.

Maybe Mya was a little bored by 2001. Although her career had been extremely successful to that point, she desired a new challenge. With maturity, she had come to understand that success and happiness can only be measured by the beholder.

She wanted to do something different. She wanted to be a bit outrageous.

Mya's next single would change her image forever. She recorded the remake of "Lady Marmalade" with the help of some of the music industry's biggest female rebels: Lil' Kim, Pink, Christina Aguilera, and Missy Elliot rounded out the roster of one of the most played songs of the year. The song was from the *Moulin Rouge* soundtrack, but did not need the backing of the film to gain popularity. In fact, the song and its video left more of a lasting impression than the musical did.

"Lady Marmalade" was unconquerable, and Mya won her first Grammy for "Best Collaboration with Vocals". The song stayed in the top 40 for nine weeks, topped the Billboard Hot 100 for five weeks, and Hot 100 Airplay chart for six weeks. During the summer months, the single proved hotter.

The "Lady Marmalade" video was at the top of the MTV Video Countdown for three weeks, and Mya won a Teen Choice Award for "Choice Song of The Summer" with the single. In September, the song was nominated for "Best Dance Video", "Best Pop Video", "Best Choreography", and "Best Art Direction" at the MTV Music Awards, and went on to win the "Video of the Year" and "Best Video from a Film" awards. Mya's life held the meaning of "Ooops I Did It Again" while Britney Spears was merely singing about it. *Mya* was the queen of the ball. Yet, despite all of the recognition that this extremely popular song had bestowed upon her, the never satisfied Mya wanted to embark on a new journey: now she wanted to try her hand as an actress.

In 2002, Mya had her first opportunity to *act* in a film rather than simply lending her vocals to the soundtrack—she had landed a role in the musical *Chicago*. Embarking on a project she had never tried before again raised many fears for Mya. She had to quell her anxiety and shyness and throw herself completely into the role. She did everything that she could to prepare for the role, including gaining weight. As usual, Mya's hard work and good decision-making paid off as *Chicago* did very well in the box office. The film also won several awards at the Golden Globes and Oscars including, "Best Musical Comedy" and "Best Film". Mya herself had enticed a new audience with her charismatic dance moves and won a Screen Actors Guild Award for her role in the film.

Mya was at the peak of her game. She had pursued what her parents knew she was to pursue when they saw her at age two in that fountain: performance. She had excelled in dancing, singing, and now acting.

Track 10: "Movin On"

Mya may have been overwhelmed, but she jumped into the development of her third release. Mya wanted a new sound for her next album and she continued to use her creativity as a stimulant for mass appeal. She knew that with the successes she had achieved, the stakes had been raised and her fans would expect a flawless project. She snagged Jennifer Lopez's former manager, Benny Medina, and began work on her project.

Two years had passed since the release of Mya's second album, and she realized that she, as well as her fans, had grown into adults during this time. Although she still wanted to appeal to young adults, she also found it necessary to entertain her adult fans with deeper music. Thus, the recording of *Moodring* began.

Mya received help on her album from IMX , a group of performers that had also grown into adults within the industry. These young men, formerly known as Immature, knew precisely how to tweak their image to appeal to a more mature crowd without ignoring the interests of their younger fans.

Mya worked on her own time schedule for the album, and found that she was truly able to perfect her art when she was not rushed. She had proved her abilities in the past as an artist and was given more control over her project by her new record label, A&M. As the album began to construct itself, she decided that its original title, *Smoke and Mirrors,* was not fitting, and used her creative control to change the name to *Moodring.*

Moodring became an album that allowed Mya to release her innate sexiness while also entertaining the audience with some of her deepest desires. Her lyrics were daring and intense. The only element that she was missing was the help of super star singer/ song-writer/rapper/creativity specialist Missy Elliot; Missy had become the key to success for a veteran artist

undergoing a change in image for today's generation. With Missy's input, *Moodring* was a guaranteed success.

Moodring debuted at number three in July of 2003 selling 112,000 copies its first week with "My Love is Like…Wo" as the first single. The song was shelved for a year prior to its release as Mya became more comfortable with its premise. It also took a considerable amount of time for her to decide to release this song as the introductory single from her album. However, the decision was rewarded as the song was nominated for two MTV Video Music Awards and reached Top 40 in August. The album went gold in September.

The album was heavily promoted as Mya appeared on television commercials, radio shows, and music award ceremonies. The excessive promotion proved to pay off as other artists' albums collapsed after their July debuts while *Moodring* continued to climb the charts.

By August, "My Love is Like…Wo" became the most talked about song of the summer. The release of this song had caused Mya to gain popularity with fans of all cultures and backgrounds. She had even become a big hit within the drag queen community, as they pumped up her songs in the hottest transsexual clubs in many urban areas.

In October, Mya continued to let her comeback be known by performing on the soap opera *Passions,* as well as at the *Vanity Fair* celebration and B.B. King's Blues Club and Grill in New York.

She explained that her image had not changed, but instead that she was simply demonstrating her versatility. As she took on new projects, the public would see just how much range Mya had.

♈rack 11: "Sophisticated ℒady"

Mya was immortalized when she lent her voice and figure to "Mya Starling", a character in the James Bond video game "Everything or Nothing". She saw this as a unique opportunity because she herself had a personal love for video games, and it was not a request that had been asked of many musicians.

She also aggressively pursued her interest in acting as she had roles in two dancing films: *Dirty Dancing: Havana Nights,* and *Shall We Dance*, starring Richard Gere and sister millennium diva of color, Jennifer Lopez. She also played the role of "Jade" in the television film *Volcano High*, and began working on Wes Craven's *Cursed*.

Through Mya's continuing success she remains a sweet, nurtured woman who treasures her family. She enjoys being alone and shies away from "star-studded" occasions. She has not flaunted her relationships with rapper 50 cent or producer Lil' Jon, nor has she let her public persona transform her personal life. Though in her professional life she is a perfectionist, she still cherishes the importance of relaxation and reflection in her personal life.

Mya long ago discovered that in order to be successful, you must be yourself and embrace your creativity. She told *Seventeen Magazine* during an interview, "I have the freedom to be who I am and who I want to be, and I'm finding myself. I like to do my own thing and trust that I'll make the right decisions. If I make a mistake, then fine. But I'm human and I have to learn for myself." She understands that maturing into the person one is destined to become is an ongoing process; it does not take place in a single moment.

Although Mya has pursued various forms of fulfilling her soul's craving for creativity, she surprisingly is not satisfied. She continues to seek new ways to express herself and ultimately, make herself happy. Through the hard times and teasing she endured throughout the years, she has come to realize that only she has control over her joy in life, and she spends every day attempting to uncover her ultimate bliss.

Outro

Without always intending to, these millennium divas of color have let us directly into their lives. Although we may follow the media's coverage of the everyday happenings in their lives, it is their music—the dearest thing to them, which truly exposes these icons.

Their albums are a cascade into their lives and souls. The album title tells us who the artist is at that particular time, while the song titles allow a more descriptive look at the woman's thoughts and experiences. The lyrics to their music are pages from their journals and from their souls—set to a beat and sang in beautiful melodies. We, the fans, have the key to every musician's diary; we *use* it when we truly listen their music.

Thus, it only makes sense that Alicia Keys titled her album *The Diary of Alicia Keys* or that Mya simply named her album *Mya*. It's simple, these albums *are* these women. Jennifer Lopez explained it best when she said, "Every album I do, I've noticed that it's really indicative of what you're going through. Who you are at that time, what kind of music you like, what kind of beats you're into, what kind of state of mind you're in, what you're attracted to…it's all very telling of where you are in your life at that point…Twenty years from now, if I give this [album] to one of my kids, I'll be like, 'This was me then, at that moment'. "

Although their music may only allow the public a momentary glimpse into their lives, their music moves us, and has a lasting effect on our spirits. We relate their experiences and emotions to events in our own lives, thereby strengthening the songs message or sentiment. The process is based on reciprocity, and is truly cathartic for the all parties involved. As fans of these "Divas of the New Millennium", we only hope that we are fortunate enough to have the opportunity to continue relating to these talented women for years to come.

Stacy-Deanne

Born in 1978 in Houston, Texas, Stacy-Deanne (Dee-Anne) is a writer of fiction and celebrity biographics. The author of *Ashanti, Jennifer Lopez* and *Mya*, Stacy-Deanne's hobbies include part-time modeling and landscape photography. She's also certified in Editing. She resides in Houston, Texas. You can learn more about Stacy and upcoming releases by visiting her official website – www.stacy-deanne.net

Kelly Kenyatta

Kelly Kenyatta is a Chicago-based writer and freelance journalist and holds a bachelor's and a master's degree in journalism. The author of *Destiny's Child*, Ms. Kenyatta has written for numerous publications including: Black Enterprise magazine, People magazine, the *Chicago Tribune, The Los Angeles Times* and the *Indianapolis Star News*. She is also the author of *Destiny's Child Complete Story; The Collector's Edition: Yes, Yes, Yes: The Unauthorized Biography of Destiny's Child (The Story of the Original 4 Members); You Forgot About Dre—The Unauthorized Biography of Dr. Dre and Eminem and Aaliyah: An R & B Princess—in Words and Pictures.*

Natasha Lowery

Natasha Lowery is the author of *Alicia Keys*. Ms. Lowery has an MFA in creative writing from the City College of New York. She has a BA in English from Fordham University. She is a native New Yorker who lived in Harlem for over 17 years. **The Alicia Keys Unauthorized Biography** is her first non-fiction work. Natasha is single and resides in Teaneck, New Jersey. She is now working on her first fiction novel.

Kwynn Sanders

Kwynn Sanders, contributing writer and editor, and author of *Beyoncé's, Kelly's,* and *Michelle's stories.* Ms. Sanders is a freelance journalist and editor residing in Pittsburg, California. She has a Bachelor's degree in English from Vanderbilt University. *Divas of The New Millennium* is Ms. Sanders first published work.

ORDER FORM

WWW.AMBERBOOKS.COM
African-American Self Help and Career Books

Fax Orders: 480-283-0991   Postal Orders: Send Checks & Money Orders
to:
Telephone Orders: 480-460-1660   Amber Books Publishing
Online Orders: E-mail: Amberbks@aol.com   1334 E. Chandler Blvd., Suite 5-D67
                                                                Phoenix, AZ 85048

——— *Divas of the New Millennium*, 0-9749779-6-9, $16.95
____ *Aaliyah—An R&B Princess in Words and Pictures* , ISBN#: 0-9702224-3-2, $10.95
____ *Michael Jackson: The King of Pop*, ISBN#: 0-9749779-0-X, $29.95
____ *Guide to Great Sex, Happiness, & Marital Bliss*, 0-9727519-2-0, $14.95
____ *50 Cent: No Holds Barred*, ISBN#: 0-9767735-2-X, $16.95
____ *Jay-Z…and the Roc-A-Fella Dynasty*, ISBN#: 0-9749779-1-8, $16.95
____ *Your Body's Calling Me: The Life & Times of "Robert" R. Kelly*, ISBN#: 0-9727519-5-5, $16.95
____ *Ready to Die: Notorious B.I.G.*, ISBN#: 0-9749779-3-4, $16.95
____ *Suge Knight: The Rise, Fall, and Rise of Death Row Records*, ISBN#: 0-9702224-7-5, $21.95
____ *You Forgot About Dre: Dr. Dre & Eminem*, ISBN#: 0-9702224-9-1, $10.95
____ *No Mistakes: The African-American Teen Guide to Growing Up Strong*, 0-9749779-2-6, $14.95
____ *Born Beautiful: The African American Teenager's Complete Beauty Guide*, 0-471-40275-3, $14.95
____ *Beautiful Black Hair: A Step-by-Step Instructional Guide*, 0-9702224-6-7, $16.95

Name:_____

Company Name:_____

Address:_____

City:_____State:_____Zip:_____

Telephone: (____) _____E-mail:_____

For Bulk Rates Call: **480-460-1660**   ## ORDER NOW

Divas of the New Millennium	$16.95
Aaliyah	$10.95
Michael Jackson	$29.95
Great Sex	$14.95
50 Cent	$16.95
Jay-Z	$16.95
R. Kelly	$16.95
Ready to Die	$16.95
Suge Knight	$21.95
Yo u Forgot About Dre	$10.95
No Mistakes	$14.95
Born Beautiful	$14.95
Hair Care	$16.95

❑ Check ❑ Money Order ❑ Cashiers Check
❑ Credit Card: ❑ MC ❑ Visa ❑ Amex ❑ Discover

CC#_____

Expiration Date:_____

Payable to: Amber Books
1334 E. Chandler Blvd., Suite 5-D67
Phoenix, AZ 85048

Shipping: $5.00 per book. Allow 7 days for delivery.
Sales Tax: Add 7.05% to books shipped to Arizona addresses.
Total enclosed: $_____

Printed in the United States
99248LV00002B/1-36/A

9 780974 977966